BACK IN MY ARMS AGAIN

by Cora Lee

For Jude, Barb, and Mary, who bring out the
best in my stories

Chapter 1

JAMES FITZSIMMONS SAT BEFORE THE fireplace in his best friend's drawing room, staring at the letters in his lap. There were three, each promising ruination and even imprisonment to the recipient should certain conditions not be met by Lady Day—the twenty-fifth of March— namely that a loan totaling the princely sum of three thousand pounds be paid in full.

The sender was the powerful Earl of Grimsby. The recipient was James's father.

"How am I going to come up with three thousand pounds in six weeks?"

Stephen Eddington settled himself on a sofa set at a right angle to James's chair, placing his elbows on his knees and resting his chin in his hands. "Well, you can't borrow against the farm."

James's father had done precisely that, igniting the fire that James was now trying to put out. "I can't ask our neighbors for help. They are comfortable, but not so wealthy they could spare this kind of money even if everyone we know contributed."

"And your father would be none too happy if they found out why he needed the money so quickly."

Because the elder Fitzsimmons had shown exceedingly poor judgment in this financial matter. Grimsby's reputation marked the earl out as deceitful and avaricious in his financial dealings, and less than gentlemanly even with the men of his own class.

James scrubbed a hand through his hair and over his face. "This would be a good time for a long-lost wealthy relative to appear and offer to make this all go away."

Eddington straightened. "That's a good idea. Not a relative, but perhaps you can find a patron who will lend you the money. I'll put up my own property as collateral if it will help."

"You're a good friend, Eddy, but I can't ask you to do that."

"You didn't ask—I volunteered," Eddington returned with a quick grin. "That, together with the ledgers from the farm for the past several years, should be enough to convince a wealthy merchant or aristocrat to lend you the three thousand pounds. Your family keeps the farm and uses some of the income from it to pay back your benefactor. No one loses their home or livelihood."

James turned the scenario over in his mind. The Fitzsimmons Farm had a long history of solid production and the documentation to prove it, so that would be an incentive to a would-be lender. It was probably the inducement his father had used to obtain the three thousand from Grimsby in the first place, though it wasn't worth that much outright. Neither was Eddington's little estate. But if they found a sympathetic ear...

"What is it?" Eddington asked, jarring James from his thoughts.

"What's what?"

"You're wrinkling your nose as if you've encountered some noxious smell. What are you thinking about that's so distasteful?"

James suppressed a sigh. "You know I don't like dealing with the aristocracy. But it appears that my family's very existence now depends on one of them."

"I did say a wealthy merchant would do as well."

"Do you know any merchants who might be willing to help?"

Eddington shook his head. "No. But I do know some aristocrats who might take pity on you."

James felt his nose wrinkle again and his mouth pull into a frown. "I don't want their pity."

"Just their money."

Ouch. But Eddy was right, and James didn't have time to be choosy. If pity was part of the bargain then he'd have to learn to live with it.

"Fine. Where do we find these soft-hearted people with large bank accounts?"

"Phillip Maitland and his wife are having a house party in a few days. They won't have the sum required, but they are well connected—Mr. Maitland is cousin to the Duke of Alston and spent some time in the Commons as an MP."

James felt his body tense at the mention of the Maitland name and the duke's title. He'd known the duke's own sister in his youth—intimately. But it had been nearly two decades since he'd last seen her, and he highly doubted she would welcome him now.

He pushed the thought aside and tried to focus on his family's current predicament. "Can we wangle a dinner invitation one evening, do you think?"

Eddington smiled brightly. "Better. I've been invited to the house party, and Mrs. Maitland just sent a note asking if I knew another gentleman that might be available. It seems she had a last-minute cancellation and needs to even out the numbers."

James hesitated. A Maitland house party? Would Cecilia be there? "Are you sure I'll be welcome? Dinner is one thing, but an entire house party is a bit more presumptuous."

"It's only a couple of weeks. And there's bound to be someone there who can help you.

Mrs. Maitland will be so glad to have an equal number of ladies and gentlemen she may even let you court her daughter."

"Two birds, one stone—how efficient. My mother would be pleased," James replied in a flat voice. She'd taken to reminding him that, while James's sister's son could inherit the farm, the boy didn't carry the Fitzsimmons name, and impressing upon James how wonderful it would be to have a grandchild that did. But Cecilia Maitland had hurt James badly the one and only time he'd proposed marriage, and at seven-and-thirty he was no longer interested in the almost political maneuverings some people undertook to make the "right" match.

"There's been no indication that Lady Cecilia will be there—she's only a distant cousin to Mr. Maitland."

James eyed his friend doubtfully. "You can't be sure of that."

Eddy shook his head. "No, I can't. But I can be sure that your farm will be in Grimsby's hands if you don't go."

"You have a point there."

"You'll go, then?"

James nodded, resigned. He could brazen out a Maitland house party in order to save the farm. And perhaps Eddy was right about Cecilia's presence there. "I'll go, and thank you for any information you can provide about the other guests."

Eddington sank back against the sofa cushions. "You're welcome to everything I know about them. Mr. and Mrs. Maitland are excellent hosts, too—you might even enjoy yourself."

James wasn't sure he'd enjoy anything until the farm was safe, but he nodded again to appease Eddington. "I might."

"You'll certainly feel better after some preparation. Come, let's adjourn to my study and we'll see what we can glean from Mrs. Maitland's invitation."

Lady Cecilia Maitland knocked on the door of her cousin's bedchamber, hoping the hour wasn't too late. Cecilia and Margaret had both been asked to arrive for the house party early to help with the preparations, and Cecilia found herself in need of counsel.

The door opened to reveal a fully-clothed Margaret Maitland, who smiled brightly when her eyes met Cecilia's. "I didn't expect to see you this late. I thought surely you'd be abed and sleeping soundly after traveling all day."

"I would be, but sleep has been rather elusive these past few nights."

Margaret took a step back and opened the door wider. "Would you like to come in for a bit? Maybe a nice chat will settle you."

"I was hoping you'd say that." Cecilia entered the room, closing her eyes momentarily to savor the heat radiating from the fireplace. There were two comfortable-looking chairs placed near the hearth, and Cecilia seated herself in the one closest to the window while Margaret took the other.

"So what has been keeping you up these past nights?"

Cecilia suppressed a smile. How very like a Maitland to get right to the point. "I've found myself in some trouble, and I'm hoping you can help me discover a way to get out of it."

Margaret's brows rose. "What kind of trouble now?"

This time Cecilia allowed the smile to form on her lips. She was the unconventional member of the Maitland family, the forty-year-old woman who set up her own household and invested her money rather than marry and depend on a husband. Being the daughter and sister of a duke meant most of the *ton* brushed off what they called her eccentricities, but Cecilia's society life had not been without incident.

But her smile faded as she spoke. "I have a blackmailer."

"What?"

"The Earl of Grimsby has an old letter of mine in his possession. One written to a lover many years ago that would disgrace me and the whole family if it became public. Or so he says."

Margaret sat back in her chair. "You doubt the existence of this letter?"

"I don't, actually. I vividly remember writing a number of letters to a certain gentleman when I was younger, so it's possible that Grimsby does possess one of them. Though I'll never know how he got his hands on it."

"You're worried about the effect on your reputation, then?"

Cecilia shook her head, her blonde nighttime plait sliding a little against her back. "I have position and wealth enough to withstand whatever backlash might occur, and I'm not exactly hunting for a husband. No, my concern is that my brother will find out."

His Grace the Duke of Alston was older than Cecilia by twelve years and had been in delicate health most of his adult life. Over the past few years "delicate" had been supplanted by "dreadful" more often than not, and the family knew it was only a matter of time before he went to his reward.

"You think the shock will be too much for him."

Margaret's voice was solemn and Cecilia gave a little nod, listening to the fire crackle cheerily along as if everything were fine.

"And you came to me because I'm no stranger to scandal."

Cecilia opened her mouth to protest, but saw that her cousin was smiling. Margaret had borne a child out of wedlock when she was nineteen and had withdrawn from Society as a result. Cecilia knew it had crushed Margaret to live as an exile in the country, particularly when she'd been so young and full of adventure. She didn't often refer to her status, but it was good to see her speaking so easily of it now.

"Because you're my favorite cousin," Cecilia returned.

Margaret chuckled. "Don't let Phillip hear you say that."

Cecilia wanted to grin and reply with some witty comment, but instead she pressed her lips together for a moment. "You can't tell anyone about this, including Phillip—the more people that know, the greater the chance someone will tell Alston."

Margaret reached across the space between their chairs and clasped Cecilia's hands in hers. "Of course I won't. Your secret is safe with me." She squeezed her cousin's hands then released them and sat back. "Now what can we do about Grimsby? What is it that he wants from you?"

"Five thousand pounds. For that I get the actual letter in addition to his silence."

Margaret's hazel eyes went round. "Five thousand?" Then she smiled. "If your investments are doing as well as they appear to be, that isn't an insurmountable sum for you. Is it?"

"No, it isn't. But that's not the point."

"You're angry that he's trying to manipulate you."

Margaret's tone was so matter-of-fact Cecilia grinned. "I'd forgotten just how well you know me. Yes, I'm angry that he thinks he can so easily move me. But I can't tell the magistrate what's happened for fear of word getting out, and Grimsby well knows it—is counting on it."

"Are you still in contact with the letter's original recipient? Perhaps you could write to him and let him know what is happening. He may even have an idea or two about how to stop it."

Cecilia pictured James as he'd been when she'd known him, tall and slim yet strong enough to lift her off the ground with little effort. He'd had a dimple in his left cheek—just a fraction of an inch from the corner of his mouth—that she'd been particularly fond of kissing. But it had been nearly twenty years since she'd seen him last, and the encounter had not ended happily.

"We lost touch," she told her cousin, which was a version of the truth. His actual words had been something more akin to *I never want to see you again.* "I suppose I could set my solicitor to searching for him, but he doesn't go about in Society."

"Then he may not care about the letter surfacing, which is just as well. I think the only thing he could really do to help is marry you. That would render the letter moot."

Cecilia nodded slowly, as if it was a simple thing Margaret suggested. Marriage to her former lover would negate the scandal the letter would otherwise cause for all but the highest sticklers, and those were people who didn't approve of her anyway. What she didn't tell Margaret was that James had been more than just a lover. He'd been a close friend, an ally, and her would-be fiancé. If Cecilia had accepted James's proposal of marriage all those years ago, she wouldn't be having this problem now.

Would she have been happier as his wife?

But what was done, was done. For all she knew, he was wed to some other woman and had a full complement of children helping him run the farm.

"Marriage to anyone would probably negate enough of the scandal that little would reach Alston, particularly if he were confined to his home or bed. I am loath to give up my independence, though, Margaret. I've been my own keeper for nigh on sixteen years now, and to sign everything over to a man feels like a defeat."

"You could retain some of your independence with the right settlements...and the right gentleman," Margaret replied with a sly smile. "And marriage would undoubtedly be more pleasurable than giving in to Grimsby."

"His lordship certainly wouldn't see it coming."

"And in a few days you'll have a house party full of gentlemen to consider."

"Half of whom I'm related to," Cecilia quipped. "But at least it's a viable action, if I want to take it. I would just have to find a willing co-conspirator."

Chapter 2

You're thinking so hard I can see smoke coming out of your ears."

"If my brain catches fire, at least we'll be warmer." James glanced over at Eddington, who was drawing his big bay gelding alongside James's dappled gray, ignoring the cloud his breath formed every time he spoke. "I'm just worried."

"Worrying isn't going to do you any good now."

Now that James had left the farm in the care of his aging parents and a brand new steward to beg the protection of some bored lord? Probably not. He just couldn't help but be anxious—there were so many things that could go wrong.

"You're sure there will be aristocrats at this house party?"

Eddington nodded, pulling the collar of his greatcoat tighter about his neck against the sleet falling like spoonfuls of freezing porridge all around them. "Phillip Maitland might not be rich and titled, but he has family and friends who are. And the Maitlands are a loyal bunch. The purpose of this house party is to give Phillip's daughter some polish before she makes her come-out this Season, so at least one of the other Maitlands will be there in a show of family support for her. And if there isn't someone at the house party that can help you directly, there will be someone who can introduce you to the right person."

James briefly wondered if the duke himself would attend. How much did His Grace know about his sister's prior relationship with a mere farmer?

"If I have to go somewhere else to beg for help *after* the house party it may be too late, especially if the weather turns ugly. Grimsby's deadline is fast approaching."

Eddy motioned toward a small stately home coming into view among the rolling Cotswold hills. "Well, let's hope there's a duke or marquess here that firmly believes in *noblesse oblige*."

An hour later James was warming himself before the fire in what was to be his chamber for the next two weeks, trying to decide the most tactful way to ask a complete stranger for a loan. A knock on the door interrupted his musings, and Eddington poked his head in.

"I have good news and bad news."

"Give me the good news first," James said, flopping down into a chair near the hearth.

Eddington took the chair opposite his friend with considerably more grace. "The Marquess of Hadleigh is here."

"And what do we know about him?"

"He's young, wealthy, and eager to prove himself a great lord."

James sat up a little straighter. "Do you think he'd be amenable to aiding an overwhelmed farmer?"

"Possibly."

"Then what's the bad news?"

The corners of Eddington's mouth turned down. "He is the only aristocratic guest. The others are well enough off, but not wealthy enough to produce three thousand pounds...except for Lady Cecilia. But she won't be useful."

James felt like he'd been punched in the chest. She was here! "Lady Cecilia?"

"Yes," Eddington answered slowly, his eyes darting around the room. "I'm sorry. I did tell you at least one member of the family would attend. Unfortunately, it turned out to be a female member with no husband to petition, and one you have a past with."

James sat in silence for a long minute, concentrating on breathing normally. He foolishly hadn't prepared himself for her actual presence, and now he had to contend with a jumble of emotions right here in front of Eddington.

"I can't borrow money from a woman," he managed at last. "And certainly not from Cecilia."

Eddington shook his head. "Of course you can't. Nor could she deal effectively with Grimsby if a problem arose."

James scrubbed a hand through his hair, trying to clear his mind by sheer force of will. "That leaves me with Hadleigh. He will undoubtedly find me vulgar if I lay out my case plainly before him and ask for his protection at dinner. You'll have to help me devise a way to sound like a gentleman when I speak to him."

They spent the next thirty minutes putting together some topics James could use when conversing with the marquess. And both James and Eddington took great pains with their appearances as they made ready for the social hour before dinner, James even allowing Eddington's valet to brush his clothing and tie his cravat.

But when they entered the drawing room at the appointed time, they found they could not locate the Marquess of Hadleigh.

"Good evening, Mr. Eddington, Mr. Fitzsimmons." Margaret Maitland greeted them each with a nod as she circulated among the guests. "I trust you are feeling well-rested this evening."

Eddington took her offered hand and bowed over it. "Indeed we are, Miss Maitland. It seems not everyone is as fortunate as we are, though. We were hoping to speak with Lord Hadleigh for a moment before dinner, but he does not appear to have come down from his chamber yet."

She took her hand back and shook her head. "Nor will he, the physician said. Not for several weeks."

"Physician?" Eddington asked.

"Weeks?" James put in, only half registering the note of anxiety in his voice.

"Did you not hear?" Miss Maitland took half a step closer. "He was conversing with my brother this afternoon," she answered in a quiet voice, "and was paying more attention to his words than to where he was going."

James winced inwardly, knowing that whatever came next was bound to be painful for both himself and the marquess.

"Lord Hadleigh fell down the staircase and broke his leg. He's confined to bed until further notice."

For the second time that day, James felt as though he'd been punched. Not only would a broken leg prevent Hadleigh from participating in house party events for the entire duration, but he would probably be dosed with laudanum to combat the pain.

He would be asleep or insensible.

And James's hopes for Hadleigh's patronage disappeared.

It was as if her conversation with Margaret had conjured him directly into her cousin's drawing room.

Cecilia spotted James from across the room. Even though it had been seventeen years since she'd set eyes on him, she recognized him easily. His hair was shorter now, but still the same golden brown it had been when she'd last run her fingers through it. His skin was not as tanned as she remembered, but his face and hands were still several shades darker than those of the other guests. His clothes were some years out of fashion, but were as neat and well-tailored as they had been during that long ago visit to London.

What was he doing here? She didn't remember his name being on the guest list Phillip's wife had shown her. Nor could she fathom how a farmer from Kent would have an acquaintance with her idle cousins in Gloucestershire.

But then again, no one would have ever guessed that the same farmer had once been very, very close to a duke's daughter.

She circulated about the room, mingling with her cousin's guests and making small talk about the usual nonsense, pretending her heart wasn't beating as though she'd danced a dozen reels. Her eyes took on a life of their own and kept darting toward James, watching as he performed the same rituals. Was he as nervous as she was? Had he even noticed she was there?

And then he was walking toward her.

Dear God in heaven, what did one say to the only man one had ever loved seventeen years after breaking his heart?

"Cousin, are you acquainted with Mr. Eddington and Mr. Fitzsimmons?"

Cecilia focused on Margaret, who was positioned between the two gentlemen as they approached, and forced herself to breathe normally. "I don't believe so. Perhaps you'll do the honors?"

Apparently, one pretended not to know the broken-hearted party at all.

Cecilia offered her hand to Mr. Eddington as Margaret made the introduction, and attempted what she hoped was a genteel smile. "It's a pleasure to have a face to put with the name—my cousins tell me you've been spending a fair amount of time here since you settled in at Westwood."

"I wouldn't say that I've settled in just yet," Mr. Eddington replied politely. "But it has been very pleasant to have neighbors as welcoming as the Maitlands."

"And Mr. Fitzsimmons," Cecilia said, turning to face James and offering her hand. He took it carefully, his brown eyes intent on her blue ones despite his relaxed expression. "I understand you have been visiting Mr. Eddington these past few days. Are you enjoying your stay in the Cotswolds?"

"I'm afraid I haven't experienced much of the region yet." He touched only her fingertips, but stroked his thumb across them before letting go. "My stay has been all business up until today."

"And what kind of business are you in?" Cecilia asked, as if she hadn't heard all the stories about his childhood on the farm.

"I am here to rescue someone," he told her. The corners of his mouth curved upward in what she recognized as his I'm-being-modest smile. "A relation got himself mixed up in a distasteful business matter, and I am attempting to keep him out of debtors' prison."

There was a Banbury tale if she'd ever heard one—who would admit that a family member was in financial trouble? But he hadn't called attention to her lie so she decided to play along with his, raising her brows and forming her mouth into a little O. "How awful," she breathed. "I do hope you are successful."

"So does his relation," Mr. Eddington replied in a rather serious tone.

Margaret's lips quirked and pressed together, as if she was trying to fight a smile. "I'm sure he does. You will let us know how it turns out, Mr. Fitzsimmons?"

"I will."

Cecilia remarked on the weather, hoping—for once—to steer the conversation into more conventional waters. Or at least to a topic she didn't have to think much about. Her mind was busy sorting out a quandary she hadn't seriously considered, despite her conversation with Margaret. Should she tell James about the blackmail? It was one thing to keep the incident to herself when his whereabouts were unknown to her, but here he was in her cousin's home, an arm's length away.

Was he still unattached? If so, would he marry her to save her brother?

Did she want him to?

James and Mr. Eddington took their leave, drifting toward a knot of gentlemen that were talking near the window. Cecilia counted slowly to five, then drew her cousin to a quieter corner of the room.

"That was him."

"Who was whom?" Margaret asked, her brows raised.

"Mr. Fitzsimmons is the man I wrote the scandalous letter to."

"The letter that Grimsby is using to extort money from you?"

Cecilia nodded, her eyes seeking out James before refocusing on Margaret. "Yes."

"He's the lover from long ago?"

"He is."

Margaret frowned. "Wait, didn't I just introduce him to you?"

Cecilia felt herself cringe. "You did. I apparently decided that it would be easier to pretend I didn't know him, or that I'd forgotten him."

"But you haven't."

Forget James? No. Even before Grimsby had dredged up old memories with her letter, James had been in her thoughts more than one would think possible after so long an absence. "Even if

I had, Grimsby's little enterprise would have brought him to the forefront again. But things did not end well between us, and I was unsure of Mr. Fitzsimmons's reaction to me."

"He seemed perfectly civil," Margaret replied. "Assuming he remains so, you now have your chance to tell him about the letter and Grimsby's use of it."

"Do you think I should?"

"The way I see it, you have three options. You can quietly pay his lordship the money he demands and get your letter back. You can come up with a plan that results in Grimsby's downfall without harming your brother. Or you can ask Mr. Fitzsimmons his opinion of the matter since, strictly speaking, he is already involved."

Cecilia smiled and touched her cousin's arm. "This is why I came to you in the first place—you can always boil a situation down to its essence. Now all I have to do is come up with a way to put Grimsby in his place."

"You won't tell Mr. Fitzsimmons about the letter, then?"

"I don't believe I will. The only reason he's involved is because his name is on the letter. If I can resolve the situation, he need never know it was an issue at all."

Margaret opened her mouth as if to reply, but was interrupted when Phillip appeared at her side holding out a piece of paper to Cecilia.

"This came in the post this morning addressed to me, but it's for us both."

"Why are you bringing correspondence to the drawing room twenty minutes before dinner?" Margaret asked, her voice a mixture of irritation and concern.

"I only just found it a few minutes ago, when I was looking for the book I wanted to lend to Mr. Hobbes. It's from Orchard Lake."

Orchard Lake was the Duke of Alston's favorite residence. Cecilia accepted the paper from her cousin and scanned it quickly. It wasn't a summons to her brother's death bed, but it wasn't a glowing report either.

"It seems His Grace has taken to his bed again," she said aloud for Margaret's benefit. "The duchess writes that while he is too weak to walk unassisted and his breathing grows ragged, he is still in good spirits with a healthy appetite. She does not want us to abandon the house party, but wishes us to be apprised of his condition in case..."

Margaret nodded. "We are apprised, then. And Her Grace will certainly inform us of any changes."

Cecilia handed the paper back to Phillip. "Thank you. You'll find me again if more news arrives?"

"Of course."

Phillip tucked the paper into the pocket of his cutaway coat, patted Cecilia's shoulder, then threaded his way across the room, presumably in pursuit of Mr. Hobbes. Cecilia's eyes met Margaret's and she suspected they were both thinking the same thing: whatever Cecilia was going to do about the Earl of Grimsby, she had better do it before he decided to make public the contents of her letter.

Chapter 3

CECILIA MADE IT THROUGH DINNER, and tea with the ladies afterward, by sheer force of will and good manners. She even managed to participate in the game of Charades someone suggested when the gentlemen joined the ladies in the drawing room. But all the while her mind was spinning, grasping at any possibility that might keep the Earl of Grimsby's mouth shut.

As soon as was polite, she said goodnight and excused herself to her bedchamber where she could move around freely while she tried to think.

"Very well then, Cecilia," she said aloud, "what can you do to keep Grimsby from telling Alston about that letter?"

The obvious answer was to pay the five thousand pounds he required and hope that he kept his promise to return the letter to her. It was the quickest, easiest way to put the whole matter to rest. But it was also predicated on a blackmailer keeping his promise.

She began walking around the room, skirting the edge of her bed and heading for the washstand before turning back toward the fireplace. "I don't like that at all. What's to stop Grimsby from refusing to turn over the letter, or demanding more money?"

She could always even the score later. Grimsby had a wife and daughter who enjoyed the entertainments of the Season, and Grimsby himself had been known to escort them about Town. With Cecilia's social position it would be easy keep Lady Grimsby's name off the guest lists for balls and soirees. A word in the ear of one of the Patronesses and vouchers for Almack's would be withheld. It would be a miserable year for a husband-hunting girl and the mother watching her flounder.

Yet it wasn't the Grimsby women that Cecilia wanted to punish, it was the earl himself.

"He might be indirectly affected, but it wouldn't be enough. And Lady Grimsby has never been anything but kind to me." Running a hand over the footboard as she passed the bed again, she shook her head and discarded the idea.

What else?

"I suppose I could arrange to have him injured."

Cecilia halted abruptly as soon as the words were out of her mouth. No, that was clearly unacceptable. She might feel justified in imagining scenarios where his lordship got what he deserved, but to actually cause physical damage would be unconscionable.

Sighing, she resumed her circuit about the chamber at a more somber pace. "I'm just going to have to pay him. My brother's peace—his very life—is certainly worth five thousand pounds. If I insist on a simultaneous exchange, the chances of getting my letter back are much greater."

Perhaps her cousin's cook would have some pastries hidden away in the kitchen that would make Cecilia's pride easier to swallow. She strode to the door and opened it, pausing in the hallway to get her bearings. As she located the main staircase, she noticed candlelight spilling out from a partially open door further down. A male voice joined the light.

"And there's no one else in a position to help, is there?"

It was James. Cecilia crept closer, gathering the material of her skirts in one hand to quiet the rustle. What was this about?

"No. I'm sorry, Fitz. I thought for sure you'd find your patron here." That was Mr. Eddington, sounding truly sorrowful. Why did James need a patron so badly?

"There has got to be a way to save the farm and keep my father out of debtors' prison. I will not give over my family's livelihood to that man, earl or not."

Keep his father out of prison? Was Mr. Fitzsimmons the relative James had cheekily discussed before dinner? And who was the earl threatening him?

Cecilia's hand went to her mouth to stifle her gasp, but it couldn't stifle her words.

"It's true, then."

James turned and found Cecilia standing just outside the partially open door, her eyes widened with surprise. He gestured her inside and closed the door tightly behind her as she entered, mentally kicking himself for not having done so in the first place.

"Yes, it's true." There was no point in denying anything now. Cecilia was an intelligent woman and he was a terrible liar—she'd see through any story he tried to concoct.

"Who is it?" Her lips pressed into a firm line and her eyes narrowed. "Wait, it's Grimsby, isn't it? He's at it again."

James turned sharply. "Why would you think that?"

"How many other blackmailing earls do you know?" she shot back.

"Blackmailing?"

Cecilia nodded. "That is what he's doing to you, isn't it?"

"Did you say 'again'?" Eddington cut in. "He's done this before?"

"He's doing it currently. To me."

The room went quiet and James tried to understand what he'd just heard. Cecilia was being blackmailed by the Earl of Grimsby?

"He has a financial hold over my father," James explained to her, glancing back at Eddington, then re-focusing on Cecilia, "It isn't blackmail, but a loan was made and now he wants full payment or we lose the farm. No one else can know. Promise me you won't breathe a word to anyone."

She nodded slowly and didn't speak for a moment. The Cecilia he'd known all those years ago would have taken a secret to her grave for him. But would she now?

Then the corners of her eyes crinkled as her mouth formed a cheerful smile. "Oh, I can do better than that—I can help you stop him."

"What? You're a woman—what can you do to an earl, a peer of the realm?"

"First of all, I have money to hire solicitors and barristers and private investigators... whatever and whoever is necessary to combat his lordship legally, if such a thing is possible. At the very least, I can pay back your loan."

"That would be helpful," Eddington said transferring his gaze from Cecilia to James. "Neither you nor I have the funds to do that."

"I also have connections to powerful lords, not the least of which is my brother."

"There's your patron." Eddington directed his words to James with a slight nod and raised brows.

"That's assuming I agree to this...this partnership. Eddington is correct in his assessment of our financial situation, but borrowing money from a female is unseemly. And what makes you think that your connections would bother with a lowly farmer you once knew? They certainly aren't going to stick their necks out because you ask nicely."

Cecilia laughed a little. "No, they probably wouldn't. But they would do anything to see justice done for a member of the family."

"Which I am not."

"You would be if we married."

Eddington made an inarticulate noise in his throat and tried to cover it with a cough. "Did you just ask Fitz for his hand?"

Cecilia kept her eyes on James. "You wouldn't be borrowing money from me, then, either—my fortune and all my investments are yours as soon as the vows are solemnized."

Eddington coughed again and James glared at him, prompting the man to excuse himself and hurry out of the room with a mumbled, "I'll just give you two some privacy."

"Marriage?" James asked, dropping into a wing chair near the fire. "We haven't been in contact with each other for seventeen years—after you declined my offer of wedded bliss, might I add. You didn't even acknowledge that you knew me before dinner today. And now you want to become my wife?"

She followed him to the fire and seated herself in the chair opposite him. "It doesn't have to be a real marriage. We would not have to live as husband and wife."

But they would still *be* husband and wife. The dream of his twenty-year-old self come true...too late. "Would your relations help me if I were just a husband of convenience?"

"Probably not," she said, clasping her hands together on her knee. "The money and my status would be yours, though, along with whatever I can do personally." She paused a moment and took a breath as if she were collecting herself. "If we told everyone it was a love match, my family would be more than happy to protect you."

James felt himself shaking his head in frustration. "Why would you even suggest such a thing? You can't love me after all these years —you don't know me anymore, nor do I know you. You can't be out to spite your relations by marrying so far beneath you, since you offered them up as allies. I'd find it very difficult to believe that you long to give up your ways as a grand lady and settle down on my farm. So what is it?"

"I treated you badly, James. I know it was a long time ago, but it still weighs on my conscience. I led you to believe we could have a life together, then cast you aside when you tried to make that a reality."

"Did it hurt you to refuse me?" he asked quietly. The pain in her voice was oddly touching, even after all the time that had passed.

Her eyes darted to his. "Of course it did. I was wounded deeply when I sent you away. That it was a self-inflicted wound made it even worse."

"Then why did you?" The words came out with more bitterness than he'd intended. "Why did you refuse me after encouraging me for months? Why did you let me think you loved me when you didn't?"

"I did love you." The words were soft, almost lost in the popping of the fire. She glanced down at her lap before meeting his gaze once again. "My niece was thirteen and not so far from thoughts of marriage herself. Marrying you, with your social rank so far below mine, would have harmed Honoria's prospects of a good match."

He let out a humorless laugh at that. "You think marrying a farmer would have rendered a duke's daughter unmarriageable?"

"Not unmarriageable, no. But I wanted her to have every opportunity to find a good husband. The scandal we would have created would have touched my whole family."

There was the real reason she'd refused him. "And they wouldn't have approved, would they?"

"No."

"Then why would they now?"

"Because I'm an old spinster," she answered flatly. "And Honoria has been safely married for over a year now. If my brother and my cousins believe marrying you makes me happy, they won't care who you are."

James stood and walked around to the back of his chair, leaning against it. "So this is your chance to atone, to make yourself feel better all these years later."

"That's part of it."

"What's the other part?"

"Grimsby also has a hold over me. He has one of the letters I wrote to you when we were together, and has threatened to make it public."

James felt his face flush with heat. Those letters had been for his eyes only, not for a snake like Grimsby and certainly not for the Society gossips.

"James?"

"I was just thinking about the things you wrote in those letters."

Pink crept into her cheeks, slowly at first then in a rush of color. "Oh."

Oh indeed. She'd poured both her heart and her physical desires into those letters.

She pressed her hands to her cheeks for a moment and cleared her throat. "I, erm, suppose I could weather the scandal well enough on my own. But I'm terribly afraid it would put too much strain on Alston's health."

"He is unwell again?"

She nodded. "I fear the stress of such humiliation would kill him. And I will not let Grimsby tear my family apart."

James leaned more heavily against the back of his chair. "I can't fault you for that. One has to protect one's family whenever possible."

"Then you agree to my plan?"

"I don't know, Cecilia." He ran a hand over the back of his neck. He didn't even know how he felt about seeing her again. How was he supposed to handle her offer to wed him?

"We can do it quickly—a marriage by special license can be arranged while we're here at the house party. Once our vows are solemnized, my letter becomes moot and you have money to save the farm. We both win, and Grimsby doesn't get to revel in our disgrace."

"We will be shackled to each other—and our past—for the rest of our lives."

"We will," she said slowly. "Though when everything has been settled, we could go our separate ways."

"How very aristocratic," he returned dryly. That was the second time she'd mentioned separate lives. Perhaps she was just as reluctant to wed him as he was her.

She sat up straighter. "You'd rather go on living together? Pretending that we can be happy together for the next thirty or forty years?" He watched her press her lips together and take another deep breath. "Let's prioritize. We can marry, safeguarding my brother, and send Grimsby a bank draft, safeguarding your farm. Then once we have that in hand and know your family to be safe, we can re-evaluate our own situation. Does that sound reasonable to you?"

James nodded, hesitant to agree but seeing no other way out of the mess his father had created. "It does."

"We'll have to make my family believe we're in love to secure their protection for you. And it will negate the need to tell them about the blackmail. Will you agree to that?"

He sighed. There really was no other way to save the farm if Grimsby went back on his word. Nor would his father appreciate James telling strangers about his financial situation. "Yes, I will agree to it."

"Then congratulations, Mr. Fitzsimmons, you and I are betrothed."

What had she done?

Cecilia lay sprawled on her bed staring up at the ceiling, wondering how she'd managed to affiance herself to a man who wanted little to do with her.

"It's for the good of us both," she told the pillow beside her. "And for our families."

The pillow was unmoved by her declaration, so she tried again. "Yes, the provision about pretending ours is a love match is necessary. News of my wedding a farmer to give him money would be at least as shocking to my brother as the letter in Grimsby's possession."

Still the pillow sat in silent judgment.

"I wasn't lying when I said our parting weighed on my conscience—I gave James every indication that I would welcome his proposal, then I refused him when the time came." She rolled onto her side and poked her index finger into the center of the pillow. "The worst part of it was that I wanted to accept him. I loved him and wanted nothing more in the world than to be his wife. But I was scared..."

"Scared of what?"

Cecilia planted her face into the pillow as Margaret closed the chamber door behind her, then flipped onto her back. "Have you forgotten how to knock?"

"I'm sorry. I heard your voice but no one else's and wanted to be sure you were well. From what I heard, that may not be the case."

Cecilia sat up and patted the bed beside her, hugging her cousin when Margaret came to sit down. "I am well enough in body, and I may have routed Grimsby. But I fear my heart is in for a turbulent month."

"What happened?"

"I am going to marry Mr. Fitzsimmons."

Margaret's lips parted as if she wanted to speak. When no words came, Cecilia filled her in on the details of the agreement she'd made with James. By the time she was done, Margaret found her voice.

"I thought you weren't going to even tell him about the letter. Why did you offer to marry him?"

"I did it on impulse. He was there before me, and in such difficulty. But he refused the help I could easily give, and I just blurted it out."

"He didn't agree with you so you proposed marriage?"

Cecilia heard the amusement in her cousin's voice and felt a smile tug at the corners of her mouth. "It sounds silly when you say it like that."

"What would you say to Honoria if she did such a thing?"

"Honoria's much more in control of herself than I am," Cecilia replied, picturing her niece at the last party they'd attended together. "She gets carried away with things from time to time, but I'm the impetuous one in the family."

"Is that what you're afraid of?" Margaret asked, taking her cousin's hand. "That you're too rash to be a wife?"

"The consequences of my actions would fall upon my husband and his family, too, not just on me. But that wasn't it." Cecilia felt her whole body tense, but forced herself to say the words. "I sent James away the first time because I was afraid of the consequences Honoria would face, but I was also afraid to live as a farmer's wife. What if I couldn't adjust to his lack of fortune?

What if I couldn't do the things I was expected to do?"

"What if you couldn't be the woman he needed?"

Cecilia leaned her head against Margaret's shoulder. "Yes."

"And now you have a safe way to find out— if it doesn't work, you go back to being Lady Cecilia without any consequences."

"And I feel like a coward all over again because of that."

Margaret put her arms around Cecilia. "Then don't think of the escape clause. Put your heart and soul into your marriage as if you were planning to live with him forever. If you're a total failure, you'll know you did the right thing all those years ago. If you're a brilliant success, then you'll vanquish your fears. Either way, you've spared your brother a blow to his fragile health and saved the Fitzsimmonses from ruin."

"Those are terms I think I can live with."

"But if you fall in love with him again..."

Cecilia shook her head against Margaret's shoulder. "It won't matter if I do. He hasn't forgiven me for the way I treated him when we were young, nor is he inclined to try."

"Then that's his loss."

"I only hope it isn't mine, too."

Chapter 4

"HERE COMES YOUR BRIDE." EDDINGTON flashed a grin at James over his plate of eggs and kippers.

James pushed his food around his own plate, glancing up at Cecilia as she entered the dining room before his eyes darted to the other guests enjoying their breakfast. "Yes, there she is."

She smiled at him, her eyes lingering on his face just a little bit longer than was strictly necessary. James managed a smile in return, but if it looked as sincere as it felt then he wasn't fooling anyone.

"You should be over the moon," Eddington continued. "You came here to find a solution to your problem and you did. Your father's name will remain unblemished and the farm will remain in Fitzsimmons hands."

"I am very relieved about that. More so than even you might realize."

"So why don't you look it?" Eddington leaned over his plate and lowered his voice. "Is it because help came from a woman? Or because help came from *that* woman?"

James put his fork down and picked up a piece of toast, contemplating the golden brown triangle. "I wasn't expecting to confront a seventeen-year-old heartbreak during my stay...or ever, really. And everything has happened so fast I've barely had time to comprehend it all."

He'd reanalyzed his past with Cecilia the previous night in the privacy of Eddy's bedchamber—how they'd courted for nearly six months, how deeply in love James had fallen, how he thought that Cecilia had felt the same way about him but walked away from the relationship when he asked for her hand. Eddington had been there for it all, his bachelor apartments just a floor above James's when they were both in Town, but saying it aloud had felt necessary.

It all seemed so long ago, but was suddenly very relevant once more.

Cecilia appeared at the table with her plate and took the empty chair beside James. "Good morning, gentlemen."

Her voice was cheerful and her blue eyes sparkled in the morning sun shining through the window. James wondered if she really was that merry or if she was just a fine actress.

Eddington responded first. "Good morning, my lady. Did you sleep well?"

"I did, actually. It took me a little while to settle down for the night, but once I did I slept like a top. How was your night, Mr. Fitzsimmons?"

"Eventful."

"Hmm, is that good or bad?"

He put the toast back on his plate, maintaining eye contact with it rather than her. "More good than bad." Finally, he raised his eyes from his plate—after all, if she was going to be his wife, he ought to be able to look her in the eye. "And there's still a lot to be done."

"Yes, there is. Can you meet me this afternoon? We can settle a number of things today."

"That will remove some of the weight from my mind."

"Good."

She reached over to touch the back of his hand but he reflexively pulled away. "Where and when shall I meet you?"

A hurt expression flickered over her face, but vanished quickly. Was she over the disappointment so swiftly or was she merely hiding it? James suddenly wished he knew.

"I'll be in Phillip's study all afternoon." Her lips curved into a smile and she leaned a little closer. "The ladies are embroidering this afternoon, so I plan to make myself scarce."

"Don't you like embroidery?" Eddington asked.

"I do, but not when there are other things that require my attention." She reached for James again, this time touching his sleeve instead of his skin. "Besides, the ladies here will spend the day talking about the upcoming Season while their fingers stitch, and gossip about who is looking for a spouse. I have no need of that kind of conversation."

She rose from the table, her plate of food still untouched, and nodded to them both before disappearing through the door.

Eddington fixed a sharp eye on James. "What was that all about?"

"I'm meeting Lady Cecilia this afternoon. Weren't you paying attention?"

"I was. Were you?"

"What do you mean?"

Eddington glanced around the room, which was empty now of all but a footman. "Aren't the people here supposed to think that you and Lady Cecilia are falling in love?"

"Yes."

"Then either your idea of love is skewed or you're a dreadful actor."

James considered that for a moment. "I know what love is. Or I did, once. I suppose I need to figure out how to show it when I don't feel it."

"Or learn to feel it."

"What?"

Eddington smiled. "Would it be so terrible to be in love with your wife?"

"In general, no. But when my wife previously decided she couldn't be married to me because I wasn't aristocratic enough, it's a bit harder to fall in love with her again."

"Maybe you don't have to."

James arched an eyebrow.

"Maybe you can summon some of what you felt for Lady Cecilia when you were younger. You don't actually have to love her, just remember how you felt when you did."

"Before or after she left me?"

Eddington sighed. "Before, of course. I remember what you were like when she refused you—possibly better than you do, given how muddled your head was then. But if you focus on the good times you two had together, you might be able to bring some of that joy into your actions now."

James thought about that for a few moments. "It makes sense...if I can ignore the way we parted."

"Can you do that?"

"I can certainly try. And I don't have any better ideas."

James went back to his breakfast with a little more enthusiasm. If he could simply remember how it felt to be in love with Cecilia —truly in love with her—this outlandish plan might actually work.

Cecilia sat at Phillip's large desk in the room he used as both his study and library, writing yet another letter in anticipation of her marriage. She'd already completed letters to her solicitor, her niece's husband, her housekeeper in London, and the Earl of Grimsby.

This letter she'd left for last, hoping inspiration would strike and writing it would be easy. It was for her brother and his duchess explaining why, after years of happy spinsterhood, she was rushing to marry a farmer. She didn't need Alston's permission, but she knew it would hurt him to learn of his only sister's marriage over tea with the neighbors.

"I'd be there to tell you in person if there was time," she said aloud.

"Perhaps we can visit when the dust has settled, so to speak."

Cecilia's eyes snapped to the doorway where James was standing, looking very confident and handsome in sharp contrast to his bearing at the breakfast table. "Would you like that?" she asked.

He entered the room and approached the desk but did not sit. "Probably as much as you would enjoy visiting my family."

"Actually, I think I should like to meet them and see the farm." She wondered briefly if that was true or if she was merely being contrary. "I certainly heard enough about both when we were courting."

His lips curved into a smile sincere enough to produce the infamous dimple. "I did go on about home a bit too much back then, didn't I? But I would be delighted to show it to you, and to visit His Grace when the time comes."

"I will add it to my list of correspondence."

James finally seated himself in one of the upholstered armchairs Phillip kept in front of the desk for visitors. "Is the list long?"

"Longer than I'd at first expected. It turns out there's more to arranging a wedding than finding a vicar and speaking vows."

"Can I help?"

Cecilia allowed herself a smile at that. The tone of his voice was one part polite helpfulness and one part hurt male pride. Now that he was resigned to their impending marriage, she suspected he wanted to take the lead.

"Yes, actually. You can start working on the terms of our settlement. I'm asking my solicitor to draw up an agreement that will include three thousand pounds for the farm loan and a clause specifying that the bulk of my estate will remain in my name, under my administration. I've also made provisions for any children we may have—"

He drew in a quick breath and tried to cover it with a cough. "Is that...a possibility?"

"It's a fairly standard clause in a marriage settlement."

"But how likely is it that we would have children?"

"If you're asking if I'm too old to bear children, the answer is no, not yet. If you want to know if I'll be sharing your bed..." She felt warmth unaccountably rise in her cheeks. Since when did talk of a little physicality embarrass her? It wasn't as though they hadn't been intimate before. "I haven't discounted the possibility. We will be married, after all."

James was silent for a long moment before speaking quietly. "Would you like to have children?"

She didn't answer right away, rising and walking around the desk as she considered. *Did she want children?* "I don't know, to be honest. I've been a single woman so long I haven't thought about becoming a mother in years." Coming to a stop in front of James, she leaned against the desk and reached for his hand, hoping for a better reaction than the one she got that morning. "What about you?"

He flinched when she touched him, but recovered quickly this time and clasped her hand in his. "I do. Though I wouldn't be devastated if it never happened. I have a nephew to dote on, and he'll inherit the farm one day. There will be other nieces and nephews that come along, too, I'm sure."

Before Cecilia realized what she was doing, she pulled James to his feet. "We agreed to tell my family we married for love, didn't we?"

She reached out and took his other hand, lacing their fingers together. "Then you need to appear as if you enjoy touching me."

His eyes widened slightly. "Do I not?"

"You didn't at breakfast."

"I used to."

She took a step closer, breathing in the scent of his shaving soap and skin. No cologne for James Fitzsimmons—that hadn't changed over the years. "Then let's see if we can bring some of that pleasure back. Or at least help us become at ease with each other again."

She released both his hands and he gave her a quizzical look in return. "What now?"

"Just touch me."

He remained still for several seconds, his eyes trained on hers. Then he slid his arms around her and drew her gently against him, his chest rising and falling more rapidly as his breathing quickened. "It's like the first swim of the summer, when the water's still chilly. If you jump in all at once, it's uncomfortable for a minute but you get used to it pretty quickly."

"That's one way to do it," she smiled, sliding her hands up his arms and resting them on his shoulders. Her heart was pounding and she was sure he could feel it, but she carried on as though she held her former lover every day. "Will you tell me about your nephew?"

"He's my sister's son, ten years old come April. Very intelligent—he's already reading up on the latest farming techniques to help increase our crop production."

She felt James's arms relaxing, his hand splayed across her back. "Do you think he'd like to go away to school? Or to university when he's older? We could set aside some money for his education."

"You don't have to do that. He may very well want to receive a formal education, but his father might not like you paying for it, particularly under the circumstances."

"Maybe we can make it a gift, then, if his parents approve." Cecilia felt his breaths begin to lengthen and slow, though his heart was pounding as hard as hers.

He bowed his head and murmured in her ear, "A gift from his Aunt Cecilia? That might be better received."

A little sigh escaped her as she tightened her arms around him, combing her fingers through his hair. When he spoke to her like that it was almost as if they'd never parted. "Then that's how we'll do it. Is there anything you want in the marriage settlement?"

"The only thing I want right now is to kiss you."

Wait, where did that come from? Had Mr. Eddington said something to James after she'd left the table at breakfast? Or was James daring her to take their pretense further? Either way, it felt good to be in his arms again even if it was a little different this time.

And she dearly wanted to kiss him. "Then do it."

His hand released her back to stroke her cheek as his lips found hers. It was a soft kiss at first and tentative, while they each relearned the contours of the other. Then the familiarity flooded back and Cecilia opened her mouth over his, deepening the kiss the way she knew he liked. He reciprocated, wrapping his arm about her once more and squeezing her bottom.

She broke away laughing. "Well, I supposed we're used to each other again."

He leaned in and captured her lips once more. "I'd forgotten how well we did that."

"You'd forgotten?"

He rested his forehead against hers. "Made myself forget. There was no use dwelling on something I could no longer have."

"Except now you can have it." She pulled him down to her and gave him one more languid kiss.

This time he broke away with a smile. "Then we might not have to make a decision about having children—it might be made for us."

"We'll see," was all she said, but her mind was whirling. She'd offered him the chance to live separate lives after their troubles were settled, but conceiving a child would change all of that.

Or would it?

"Do you think your family will believe we're marrying for love?" he asked in a low voice.

"Think of these kisses every time you look at me, every time you touch me, and no one will ever believe otherwise."

He dropped a kiss on the tip of her nose. "Then that's one thing we no longer have to worry about. Shall we get your letters finished up?"

He released her and dropped back into his chair. The distance between them felt strange after being pressed against each other, but she rounded the desk and took up her pen as she resumed her seat.

"*Is* there anything you want in the marriage settlement, James?"

His body sagged, as if the air had been let out of him. "No. Have your solicitor draw up whatever document you think is best, and I'll sign it. I only want to keep my farm and my family safe."

Chapter 5

Two weeks later, James once again sat with Cecilia discussing their impending wedding. This time, though, they were seated side by side on the sofa in the drawing room of her Hanover Square home in London.

"Is everything at Mivart's to your satisfaction?"

She'd made arrangements for him to stay at Mivart's Hotel, just a few minutes' walk down Brook Street, until the ceremony. "Very much so. And Eddington asked me to pass along his gratitude—it was very generous of you to secure a room for him as well."

"I thought it would be easier for you if you had a friend here."

James found himself biting back a grin. "My brother-in-law said the same thing to my sister when they were wed. She traveled to his parish church for the ceremony, with my parents and I to follow a few days later. She was so nervous, her betrothed suggested she bring a cousin or close friend to keep her company."

"You were never the skittish type, though."

"I'm not now, either." And that was the truth. James might have misgivings about what he and Cecilia were about to do, but the settlements had been signed and the special license issued. His family's livelihood would be safe in a matter of days, and he wasn't about to jeopardize that.

She smiled and turned toward him, resting her elbow on the back of the sofa. "I expected nothing less."

He reflexively reached for the hand that rested in her lap and gave it a squeeze. Two weeks of pretending intimacy—or as near to intimacy as two people can get with a group of guests at a house party—had made the gesture almost automatic. "I do have a whole new appreciation for would-be brides, though, particularly the younger ones. Everything is arranged for them, and not just the ceremony.

Their whole future is settled by their fathers and husbands-to-be."

"Women often give up a lot for marriage, but they often receive a lot in return."

"You said 'they.' You don't count yourself one of them?"

Cecilia shook her head, the blonde curls at her temples swaying gently with the motion. "I'm in a very different position than most women. I'm giving up only my name and a little money for our marriage."

"You are giving up your name, aren't you? For some reason it hadn't occurred to me before now. Cecilia Fitzsimmons does have a nice ring to it."

She gave a rather unladylike snort. "You said you sympathize with brides now, perhaps you should change your name. James Maitland sounds lovely."

He must have given her an odd look, for she adjusted her grip on his hand and explained further. "Sometimes when a man marries an heiress or a lady with a title of her own, one of the conditions in the settlement is that he take her name, or that they hyphenate both their names. It's meant to keep her family name from becoming subsumed by his, when it was her money or title in the first place. It doesn't happen often, but it does happen."

"Is that something you'd want? I don't have a lot to give in this marriage, but I can give you your name."

She didn't reply right away, casting her eyes downward for a moment before returning her gaze to his. "Thank you for that. I don't need to keep my name, but I very much appreciate you considering it. Most men would laugh at the very idea."

He leaned slightly forward. "I'm not most men."

"That's one of the reasons I'm marrying you."

"Is it?" He felt his eyes widen in surprise. "You never mentioned it before."

"You think I'd offer up my family and fortune to just anyone?"

She shook her head again, and James was taken by the sudden urge to wrap one of her curls around his finger. But that act hadn't been part of their repertoire at the house party.

Nor was there anyone in the house to impress with their faux devotion to each other.

Yet here they sat, holding hands and sharing confidences.

He gave in and let himself tug a lock of her hair gently through the fingers of his free hand. "You don't have a past relationship with just anyone, either. Do you?"

The distance between them doubled without warning. "James Fitzsimmons, what kind of woman do you think I am?"

"That's just it, I don't really know." He slid closer and clasped her hand again, wanting even that little bit of skin to skin contact with her. "I didn't mean to imply that you were anything but a proper lady. But you were so warm and open with me, I thought perhaps you'd found someone else to share that with."

"Only you. You had a way of making me feel important, James, and not because of who my relations are. And you made me feel comfortable enough to let my guard down. Few people have been able to do that."

"So I'm definitely not most men," he smiled, taking her other hand in his. "You are certainly not most women. You made it easy to forget that our stations were so much different, to just enjoy my time with you and be myself."

She smiled softly. "That bodes well for our marriage, then. I know things between us will never be what they were, but perhaps we can at least be friends again."

Friends who also wanted to bed each other. Cecilia had told him to keep in mind the kisses they'd shared in Phillip Maitland's study to help sell their new relationship, but James had had trouble *not* thinking about them. With her lips on his skin now he abruptly understood how blood could run hot, and his mind filled with images of the two of them tangled in crisp linen sheets. Tomorrow was going to be their wedding night. And they had discussed having children...

But no. A physical relationship with Cecilia was not a complication he needed. Better to remember his family, waiting for news back in Kent, and focus on taking care of them.

"I think I would like us to be friends again." To his surprise, he meant it. He still hadn't forgiven her for casting him aside so easily before, but her efforts toward securing his family and the farm had begun to melt his resolve. And things would certainly be easier between them if they could forge a friendship.

The carriage clock on the mantle chimed the hour and Cecilia released his hands. "You should probably go. The neighbors, no doubt, took careful note of your arrival and will be watching with great anticipation for your departure. You wouldn't want to ruin my reputation, would you?"

The question was asked with a wink and James grinned. She used to say much the same thing to him when they were younger, meeting in secret. "No, my lady, I certainly wouldn't."

He bowed over her offered hand, wondering if the kiss he placed on her fingertips heated her blood as much as her kiss had heated his. If she felt anything she gave no outward sign, but James headed back to his hotel with more vigor in his step than he'd had in some time.

Cecilia's wedding day was cold but sunny. The vicar arrived fifteen minutes early, but fortunately so did her niece Honoria, husband in tow, and the four of them settled in the drawing room with tea and coffee to await the bridegroom.

"Congratulations, Aunt," Honoria said, wrapping her arms around Cecilia. "I'm so happy for you."

"Happiness abounds for the Maitland women this winter," Cecilia replied, hugging her niece tightly, then hugging Benedict, too. "How is my little great-niece?"

Benedict's smile reached almost literally from ear to ear. "As lively as her mother."

Honoria laughed. "She mostly sleeps and sucks on her fingers."

"That's mainly what you've been doing since she was born," he replied. "Minus the finger-sucking, of course."

"If you'd been through what I went through to bring that child into this world, you'd need a lot of rest, too," Honoria said, swatting his shoulder.

He caught her hand and kissed it quickly before releasing it. "It wasn't a criticism, my love. Merely an observation."

Cecilia couldn't help but smile at the two of them. She'd wondered for a long time if Honoria might follow in her own spinster footsteps, but the girl had simply been waiting for the right gentleman to come into her life. Or back into her life, in this case. Honoria and Benedict had known each other as children and only later discovered romantic feelings for one another.

Cecilia briefly considered a possible parallel between her own situation and her niece's, then dismissed it. Benedict and Honoria had parted amicably when Benedict sailed away to Greece to assist Lord Elgin in his preservation of the statuary there, but Cecilia's parting from James hadn't exactly been on good terms. They did rub along fairly well together at the house party, though. And those kisses in Phillip's study...

The butler announced James's arrival and Cecilia smiled as he entered the room. He was dressed in cream breaches and a green tailcoat that matched the leaves of the flowers embroidered on his cream waistcoat. She held out her hands to him, glad she had chosen an evening dress of rose silk rather than the plainer day dress she'd originally thought to wear.

"Mr. Fitzsimmons."

He took her hands in his and kissed them both, his lips soft against her skin. "Lady Cecilia."

Mr. Eddington entered behind his friend and Cecilia introduced them to the assemblage before gathering everyone in front of the fireplace for the ceremony. The vicar took his place before the couple and began the ceremony. Words were spoken and promises made, then James slid a polished gold band onto Cecilia's finger.

"I pronounce that they be man and wife together, In the Name of the Father, and of the Son, and of the Holy Ghost. Amen."

And just like that, she and James were joined together for the rest of their lives.

Honoria was the first to embrace her, whispering more good wishes into her aunt's ear. But when she released Cecilia, Honoria reached for James.

"Welcome to the family, Mr. Fitzsimmons," she told him cheerily as she hugged him. "Or might I call you Uncle now?"

The color rose in James's face, tinting his skin a pink that was only a shade or two lighter than Cecilia's gown. "You may call me Uncle if you wish," he murmured, slipping his arms around Honoria for a moment.

"Honoria, would you show the gentlemen into the dining room? The staff have prepared a scrumptious wedding breakfast—"

"—and the happy couple would like a moment alone," Honoria finished with a wink. She accepted the arm Mr. Eddington offered her and led Benedict and the vicar from the room.

Cecilia turned to James and took his hand. "Thank you for allowing my niece some latitude. I am her father's only sibling and her mother was an only child, so she had no uncles until today."

To her relief, James flashed a smile. "Well, I had no nieces until today. It may take some getting used to, but I suspect I will enjoy the addition to my family."

Cecilia stepped closer and lowered her voice. "Speaking of family, I instructed one of the footmen to carry a message to my man of business as soon as the ceremony had concluded. Payment is being delivered to Grimsby this afternoon, with instructions to have my letter returned to this address. By the time we retire for the evening, everyone will be safe from Grimsby's schemes."

James took her in his arms and held her tightly against him. "Thank you," he whispered, kissing her hair.

She let herself lean against him, breathing in the woodsy scent of cedar he wore. Interesting that he'd chosen to wear cologne this day, particularly one that brought their former favorite trysting place so easily to mind. "It's my pleasure, Husband."

He kissed her hair once more, then she felt his warm lips on her temple, her earlobe. "May I show you my gratitude, Wife?"

She raised her face to his. "And be the first to kiss the bride? Yes, you may."

His mouth found hers with a passion they hadn't shared in nearly twenty years, his hands slowly traveling down her back to cup her bottom. She draped her arms around his neck held him as tightly as he held her, wishing there weren't so many layers of clothing between them.

Wishing there weren't people waiting for them in the dining room.

She broke away reluctantly, keeping her eyes closed as she tried to steady her breathing. "You must be *very* grateful indeed."

His lips brushed her cheek, the corner of her mouth. "Apparently I am."

Cecilia blinked open her eyes and studied his face. "You sound surprised."

"Not surprised to be grateful," he replied softly. "A little surprised by the zeal with which I expressed myself."

"We always had zeal, didn't we? I could send our regrets to our guests and we could find out how much more zeal we can awaken."

He kissed her again, more gently this time, as if they were already ensconced in their bedchamber and had all the time in the world.

"No, we should celebrate with them and eat that wonderful meal your staff prepared."

She nodded. He was right, of course. Spending time being affectionate newlyweds in front of guests would help cement the idea of a love match in Honoria's mind, and that would be critical in convincing her father. And becoming physically intimate when they were unsure of each other emotionally was a disaster waiting to happen.

"We'll need our strength if we become as ardent as we used to." He dropped one last kiss on her lips and squeezed her bottom before releasing her.

Cecilia allowed her husband to escort her from the room, her head as fuzzy as her skin was hot. Was James teasing her? Had he purposefully aroused her only to leave her wanting?

Or did he mean to give her the wedding night she'd dreamed of all those years ago?

Chapter 6

It WAS ANOTHER WEEK BEFORE James resided in the same chamber as his wife—a week in which he was by turns pleased and frustrated that he kept his body from dictating his actions. As much as he wanted to bed Cecilia, he knew that engaging in marital relations would complicate their already knotty relationship—especially if they conceived a child together.

And the last thing he needed was another complication before meeting the Duke of Alston.

James stood in front of the pier glass in the chamber the newlyweds had been given at Orchard Lake, looking for imperfections in his clothing and person. He could hear Cecilia murmuring to her lady's maid in the adjoining dressing room and wondered if she had the same jittery feeling that was growing in his limbs.

The image of the lady's maid appeared in the glass, and James turned just in time to see her disappear through the chamber door. Cecilia appeared a moment later clad in a pale blue gown that fairly floated around her.

She approached him and brushed imaginary dust from his shoulders. "Nervous?"

"Is it so obvious?"

"No, that's why I asked," she replied, turning him around to face the glass once again. "You look calm and confident."

Her blue eyes peeked over his shoulder and he met her reflected gaze. "Good. Those are qualities I want your brother to associate with me. I've never met a duke before, and I am now related to this duke because of some less than savory circumstances. The blackmail, I mean," he added quickly.

"Blackmail certainly qualifies as less than savory." He could see the corner of her eyes crinkle in what must have been a smile. "Though Alston doesn't know about that part."

"That should help."

She tugged gently at the hem of his coat and smoothed out the tail. "Do you remember when we first met and you found out I was *Lady Cecilia?*"

"I immediately wondered what I'd got myself into."

"You could have turned tail and run, but you didn't."

"I was already besotted with you," he replied slowly. "I didn't want to run."

She stepped beside him and threaded her arm through his. "Do you want to run now?"

"No." He was pleasantly surprised to hear strength in his voice.

"Good. Alston likes to be shown the deference he is due as a duke, but hates being treated like an invalid—even when he is one. It's a fine line to tread, but you managed it with me."

Cecilia had made it clear all those years ago that she expected a certain level of conduct from him, but she'd also maintained that her relations' interests weren't necessarily her own. James had responded by acknowledging her social station to be above his while ignoring the implications of her surname.

Perhaps a similar approach would work with His Grace as well.

"Let's go and find out."

They entered the drawing room arm-in-arm and approached Alston, who was ensconced in a rather throne-like chair upholstered in cream with gilt carvings forming the supports and legs. He was dressed in expensively tailored clothing and looked ready for action, but James could hear His Grace's labored breathing over the rustle of Cecilia's gown.

Alston remained seated and held his arms out to his sister. "Dearest Cecilia, how glad I am that you've come."

"How wonderful it is to be here," she returned, bending to embrace him and kiss his cheek. "It feels like ages since we were last together."

"It was so long ago you were a different person."

Cecilia straightened, but didn't stiffen as James thought she might. "My name may have changed, brother dear, but I am still very much myself."

Alston's lips curled into a smile. "Of course you are. And this must be your new husband."

James executed a bow slightly deeper than was necessary in the drawing room of a close relation. "Your Grace, it's a pleasure to finally meet you."

"And you." Alston gave a shallow bow from his chair and gestured to the lady seated on the sofa nearest to him. "My wife, the Duchess of Alston."

James took his new sister-in-law's offered hand and kissed the air just above it. "Your Grace."

She inclined her head even less than Alston had, but she was smiling. "It's so wonderful to meet the gentleman who finally enticed our Cecilia into wedded bliss."

Is that what his wife had told her family? Well, James wouldn't contradict her—not after she'd fulfilled her side of their bargain with such speed. "It took seventeen years, but now we have the rest of our lives together."

The duchess sniffled and blinked as if she were holding back tears, yet she was smiling brightly. "I'm so glad for the both of you."

Cecilia was invited to sit beside her sister-in-law, while His Grace beckoned James to pull a chair up beside the ducal "throne." He did so, bracing for the grilling he expected to receive.

Alston leaned over the arm of his chair and lowered his voice. "Did you marry my sister for her money, Mr. Fitzsimmons?"

How was James to answer that truthfully without betraying Cecilia? "Her solicitor drew up a marriage settlement that kept her money under her own control, and my farm is very profitable. If my wife ever invests money in the farm—or anything else—it will be her own decision."

Alston sat back with a satisfied smile. "I assumed she would make such an arrangement, but as her older brother it is still my duty to protect her whenever possible. Since that business is settled, we may now speak of much more agreeable matters. Are you interested in music at all?"

Dinner that evening was a quiet family affair, held in the morning room rather than the formal dining room. Alston had required help to rise from his chair in the drawing room, and was slowly escorted by his wife and a burly footman to his place at the table. Cecilia and James had trailed behind, seating themselves across from her brother and sister-in-law in a cozy little square.

But midway through the first course His Grace began coughing, and by the time the second course was being served his labored breathing had escalated into persistent wheezing.

"Darling," the duchess said sweetly, laying a hand on her husband's shoulder. "Perhaps you'd better retire for the evening."

Alston glared at his plate and forced a slow breath in through his nose. But his expression softened when he looked at Her Grace and coughed in lieu of an exhalation. "Perhaps you are right, my dear. Would you..."

James sat in awkward helplessness as two footmen came to assist Alston from his chair and out of the room, wheezing and coughing all the way, while the duchess conferred with a maid.

"Should we do something?" he asked Cecilia in a half-whisper.

She shook her head. "Not yet. The footmen will take Alston to his bedchamber, and Her Grace will get him settled."

His wife not his valet? Interesting.

"My husband will want me to apologize on his behalf," the duchess said, turning to James and Cecilia. "He had so hoped to make it all the way through dinner with the two of you."

"He cannot control his illness," Cecilia replied with a wave of her hand. "If he could, he would have forced its submission to him long ago."

"That's true enough," the Duchess of Alston smiled. "Please enjoy the rest of the meal. When Alston is recovered enough for company, he will no doubt send for you."

She disappeared through the same door her husband had been carried through, and James looked at his wife. "So we're just supposed to sit here and eat as if nothing happened?"

"Eat, yes. Pretend as if nothing happened, no. Of course you can't go on as if you didn't just see your new brother-in-law fighting for every breath he took."

And if it was difficult for James, how hard must it be for Alston's own sister? He reached over and clasped Cecilia's hand, running his thumb over the back. "Nor can you."

"I will manage."

"But you don't have to manage alone. Not anymore."

She didn't respond with words, but her fingers curled around his hand and gripped it tightly. They sat in silence for several long moments that should have been awkward—but oddly weren't—as her throat worked and her eyelids blinked.

Then she cleared her throat and kissed his hand. "Thank you," she said softly. "I don't believe I'm hungry after all. Would you mind terribly if we retired to our chamber?"

She'd said *we* not *I*, and for the first time since leaving his farm, James felt useful again.

Needed. "Of course. Perhaps a little reading by the fire will settle us both."

An hour later, they were fetched by a footman to the ducal bedchamber with little fanfare and no context. Were they to say their last goodbyes to His Grace? Cecilia seemed heartened by the summons, though, and when they entered the large room James understood why.

Alston was sitting up in bed, propped up by a mountain of pillows and still laboring for breath, but with a little more ease than at dinner. He was clad only in his shirt and trousers, his discarded clothing being scooped up by a man who was probably the duke's valet. Her Grace sat beside him on the counterpane, leaning against an identical set of pillows as she read aloud from a book that sounded like a farming treatise.

"Ah, there you are," the duchess smiled as Cecilia led James deeper into the room.

Cecilia smiled at her sister-in-law, but directed her question to her brother. "How are you feeling, Alston?"

"Ready for another cup of coffee," came the reply. His voice was weak and wheezy, but steady, and he held out his arms for the embrace Cecilia offered.

Her Grace started to slide off the big bed, but Cecilia stopped her. "I'll get it. This is the tray over here?"

To James's surprise, his wife crossed to the silver tray and poured out two cups of coffee, adding cream and sugar to one before serving the duke and duchess with her own hands. "James, would you like a cup? It's strong, because that seems to help calm Alston's breathing. But I can ring for tea if you'd rather have that."

"Coffee will be fine, thank you," he murmured.

Alston gestured to a chair next to his side of the bed. "Come and sit here, Fitzsimmons. I've a thing or two I'd like your opinion on. My home farm has been struggling to produce these past few years, and Cecilia says you're an expert on such matters."

Her Grace shot a warning look at Alston. "You know talking only exacerbates your condition."

"Then I shall do most of the talking," James supplied with a smile, taking the indicated seat. "Cecilia tells me I can discuss farming until long after everyone has stopped paying attention."

Cecilia appeared beside James, handing him a cup with her brows raised slightly. Was she remembering the last time she'd poked fun at his agricultural ramblings? It had been just days before he'd asked for her hand.

"It's true," she replied, running a hand over James's back after he'd taken his cup from her. "I have never met a man so passionate about any one thing."

James forced himself not to react. That had been the other half of their private joke—that Cecilia was the only thing he was more passionate about than his livelihood. Her hand came to rest on his shoulder and he dared a quick look up at her. A small smile played on her pink lips and her blue eyes crinkled slightly at the edges.

Was she remembering the demonstration of James's passion that had followed?

"Cecilia, my dear, perhaps you could convince my lady wife to take some air," Alston said, shattering the moment. "It isn't good for her to always be cooped up here with me."

Cecilia gave her husband's shoulder a squeeze, trailing her fingers down his arm as she moved toward the duchess. "Of course. How does a walk in the garden sound?"

Her Grace took a long look at the duke, pressing her lips together before answering. "A short one will do us both some good, I imagine," she agreed, pushing herself off the bed. "The cold air will clear our heads."

The ladies departed, and Alston met James's gaze. "My duchess works too hard tending me, but she won't leave me to the care of our servants." His words were slow and somewhat hoarse, as if he'd been shouting all evening. "I'm glad you and Cecilia are here now, though I'd have preferred to be in better health for our first meeting."

James stared, taken aback by the pronouncement. He'd have thought an aristocratic family like the Alstons wouldn't have dirtied their hands in a sickroom. But here was the duchess herself having to be persuaded to leave.

"Perhaps Cecilia will remind Her Grace to look to herself a bit more."

Alston nodded. "It's easier for her to leave me in the company of family, too. Even new family."

"But I'm a stranger yet." James hoped his eyes hadn't widened as much as he feared they had.

"Yes and no," the duke replied. "It's true Her Grace and I don't know you well, but we know Cecilia and we trust her judgment. And if Cecilia thinks you worthy of her hand, we are content to believe so as well."

He shifted on the bed as if he hadn't just turned James's world on its side, trying to adjust one of the pillows at his back. "Now, would you please tell me what can be done to improve my home farm?"

Chapter 7

"WHAT DID THE TWO OF you end up discussing?" Cecilia asked, draping herself across the big bed in their bedchamber. She was still fully clothed, but her spirits were low and her body drained. The soft feather mattress would go a long way toward alleviating at least one of those problems, and she hoped a light conversation with her husband would take care of the other.

James moved quietly about the room, shucking his tailcoat and unwinding the cravat from his neck. "Irrigation. From what your brother described, his crops are either drenched or parched—he can't seem to regulate the amount of water they receive. We talked about some different things that could be done to fix that."

She'd been focused on the elaborate plaster ceiling above her, but lolled her head to one side and smirked at James. "Sounds exciting."

"It was, actually," he grinned back. "Solving a problem always gets my heart pumping."

Could that have been why he was so amorous after their wedding? A serious problem had been solved that day for both of them.

She brushed the thought aside. "Then it did you both some good. Alston was considerably more cheerful when Her Grace and I returned."

He hadn't sounded any better with all that wheezing punctuating his every breath, but he'd been smiling when the ladies reentered his chamber. And Cecilia couldn't remember the last time she'd seen her brother smile during one of his attacks.

"What about you?" James draped his cravat over a chair with his coat and hoisted himself onto the bed beside her. "Did your walk cheer you?"

"A little." She'd felt more relief than anything at the chance to escape the sickroom and the helplessness that dwelled there.

Not that she'd admit that to anyone.

James turned onto his side and met her gaze, brushing a blonde curl from her face. "How long has your brother been ill?"

They'd discussed Alston's health at length once upon a time, but perhaps James had forgotten. "He first began to notice symptoms not long after he left university, and slowly declined from there."

"You were still just a girl, then."

Cecilia had been ten years old the first time her brother had his first attack, and younger still when he'd complained of those first symptoms. "I was. Alston has been unwell for most of my life."

The statement hit her like a cricket bat. How had she never realized that before?

Her surprise must have shown on her face because James reached over and clasped her hand, giving it a gentle squeeze. "Did that, perhaps, influence you as you grew older?"

What was he driving at? "Quite possibly. There were many times we had plans to travel here or there, or to participate in some event or other, and had to make last-minute changes because of Alston's health." She drew here eyebrows down as she thought back to her childhood. "It was never something we talked much about as a family. We just did it."

"You and your parents protected him."

She nodded. "I suppose we did."

"And that's why, when I asked for your hand all those years ago, you declined. Because protecting your family is quite literally second nature to you."

Cecilia studied his face, his skin darker against the cream-colored coverlet, his mouth curving upward very slightly. "Perhaps it is."

He drew her hand to his lips and pressed a kiss to her palm. "I didn't see it before. I'm sorry, Cecilia."

"You can't mean to tell me that you'd have taken my refusal with a smile had you known me better."

He dropped their clasped hands onto the bed between them and pressed his lips together for a long moment before speaking. "Not with a smile, no. But I may have spent less energy being angry with you afterwards."

"How angry were you?" The words slipped out in a near whisper. She hadn't meant to ask the question aloud, but she was burning to know his answer. How much had he hated her?

"Too angry," was all he responded, his voice not much louder than hers, "for much too long. But I'm not any longer. I would do anything to protect my parents, my sister and her family, no matter how painful. That's what you did for Alston, for Honoria... I understand that now."

Tension she'd carried in her heart for seventeen years finally eased, and Cecilia felt her body relax into the feather mattress. She sat up, releasing his hand and stroking his cheek as she looked down into his bright eyes. "I'm so glad, James. Truly."

There was another pause in the conversation while their gazes met and held. This was the same James she'd fallen in love with as a young woman, and she had no words to describe how good it felt to have him back.

"Now," he said, clearing his throat and breaking the moment. "When was the last time someone did something for you?"

She chuckled. "You've seen my home. Do you not remember the servants there? Or here, for that matter?"

"That's not what I mean." He snaked an arm around her body and drew her down to him, smiling up at her when she halted herself with a hand to his chest. "When was the last time someone close to you offered you comfort? Alston has his duchess and his children, and Her Grace has you. But you've had a rather fretful day yourself."

"And you're offering to comfort me?" The tip of one finger had landed just inside the open neck of his shirt, and she drew a small circle on his exposed skin. His chest rose beneath her hand as he inhaled sharply.

"If you wish it."

A part of her wanted to peel the remaining clothes from his body and spend the rest of the evening reacquainting herself with its contours. But worrying over Alston and trying to keep up a brave front for her sister-in-law had been exhausting, and her brother was still in danger. Instead, she slid her arm around him and nestled herself against his chest, tucking her head beneath his chin.

"Would you hold me for a while? We can talk or not as you please, but I would very much like your arms around me."

James obliged, planting a kiss on her hair as they sought a mutually comfortable arrangement of their bodies. "My arms are at your disposal. And not just tonight. No matter what happens between us, if you should ever need me—for anything at all—you need only ask."

She turned her head slightly and pressed her lips to his skin, to the same place her fingertip had been. "Thank you, James. That means a great deal to me."

They fell silent once more and Cecilia closed her eyes, allowing the slow rise and fall of his chest to lull her into a dreamless sleep.

When she blinked open her eyes, the bedchamber was dark and James had disappeared. Cecilia rubbed her eyes and sat up, noting that the room wasn't completely dark—there was a fire burning in the fire place. As her vision adjusted to the gloom, the outline of a man came into focus. He was sitting in a chair practically on the hearth, trying to catch the firelight on a piece of paper.

Stretching as she slid off the bed, she crossed the room to join her husband. He looked up at her approach and offered a smile.

"I thought you might sleep all night in your gown and shoes."

His body was turned toward the fire and Cecilia positioned herself behind him, resting her hands on his shoulders. "Is it very late?"

"Nearly midnight."

"You could have woken me."

James shook his head, laying a hand over one of hers. "Extra sleep never hurt anyone. And I suspect you needed it."

"I did," she replied, realizing the truth of her words as she spoke them. Between her brother's health and Grimsby's blackmail, the past few weeks had been more distressing than she'd realized. "What about you? Did you sleep?

"No. I couldn't stop thinking about these." He held up the letter he'd been reading and its companion, folded but with a broken seal.

"From the farm?"

He nodded, glancing down at the paper in his hand.

She slid her arms down his chest and lightly embraced him. "All is well, I hope."

James rested his cheek against hers, and she felt him smile for the briefest of moments. "It seems to be. My father has confirmed everything the steward has reported..."

His voice trailed off, and Cecilia kissed his cheek. "But you wish you were there to see it with your own eyes."

He inhaled deeply and let the breath out on a sigh. "Yes, I do."

"We can—"

"No need," he interrupted. "At least, not yet. Your brother needs you more than my farm needs me right now."

Cecilia tightened her arms around him, dropping another kiss on his cheek. "Thank you. I want to meet your parents, your sister and her family, but I'm reluctant to leave here."

He unwrapped her arms from his shoulders and led her around the chair, snaking an arm around her waist and drawing her onto his lap. "They will be pleased to meet you, and not just because you saved the farm. I think they'll like you."

She dropped her head to his shoulder and smiled, hoping the low light of the room masked the anxiety that suddenly welled up inside her. "I hope so."

"I can't, however make any promises on behalf of our animals," he laughed. "We have one old cow who has appointed herself guardian of the others..."

She felt her body tense and James's voice trailed off. He ran one of his large hands up and down her arm in a gesture that she thought was meant to be reassuring. "But I don't want you to feel like you have to work when you're on the farm. You won't have to deal with the livestock—"

"James." She lifted her head from his shoulder and met his gaze. "Might I confess something to you?"

"Of course."

His eyes were wide in the firelight, his brows raised in silent question. Would he be angry? Would he judge her to be just another spoiled aristocrat?

There was only one way to find out.

"I am terrified of visiting the farm."

His brows rose even higher, but his hand began rubbing her arm again. "What? Why?"

Cecilia wanted to bury her face in his shirt so she didn't have to look at him, but she forced herself to maintain eye contact. "I have only the most rudimentary knowledge of farms in general, and only old stories of your farm in particular. I am afraid that, not only would I be completely useless, but that I would actually hinder operations."

He smoothed her cheek with roughened fingertips, grinning. "Cecilia Fitzsimmons, a hindrance? Never."

"I'm serious, James. I was trained to dance at balls and converse with strangers. I know nothing about cows or crops."

His hand dropped from her face and his smile faded. "I'm sorry. I didn't mean to poke fun at you. But you are the least useless woman

I have ever known, and I was trying to picture you bumbling about the stables and fields. The vision was so incongruous with your actual capabilities, I couldn't help but smile."

"What capabilities?" she asked pointedly. "I have no skills that would be useful on a farm."

"You are an excellent manager of people," James replied, the corners of his mouth turning up once more in a smaller smile. "That is enormously useful on a farm such as mine that is worked by a small army. There are always more tasks to be done than can be completed in a day, and someone needs to keep track of which tasks are completed by which people and how well it is done. I saw you do the very same thing at your home in Town."

"Of course I did—that's called managing a home. But your farm doesn't have a butler or housekeeper."

"No, but it does have a steward."

He had a point there. The role of property steward was not unlike that of a housekeeper, and Cecilia had dealt with housekeepers for years. "Are you going to keep him on after you return?"

It was only after she'd asked the question that she realized how full of meaning it was. James wouldn't need to retain the steward if he planned to remain in residence once he returned to the farm. And if James wasn't leaving, that meant Cecilia would be traveling about the country alone, separate from her husband.

Separated from her husband?

"I don't know." James sighed again. "I've spent my whole life on that farm, *given* my whole life to that farm. I love it as much—" He stopped abruptly and dropped his gaze to her lips. Then he cleared his throat and raised his eyes to hers "—as much as I love my family. And it hurts to leave it in the care of another. But I have also enjoyed my time away, being something of an idle gentleman for a few weeks while I spend time with you."

He liked spending time with her, away from his work. Her younger self would have swooned to hear such words from her dedicated farmer. Her current self couldn't help but smile broadly. "Speaking of idle time together, may I ask you one favor before we descend upon your family?"

"Ask away."

"Would you come with me to London when we leave here? From there we can go directly to the farm and stay as long as you wish. But I'd like very much for you to escort me to a ball when the Season opens."

His entire face seemed to frown. "A ball?"

"Just one, given by Benedict's cousins every year. Grimsby will undoubtedly be there—everyone is—and I'd like to have a word with him. In public."

She winked with her last statement and James laughed. "I see. Well, I can't fault you for that."

"You might even take pleasure in it." She leaned in close, her mouth just a fraction of an inch from his ear. "As much pleasure, perhaps, as I will seeing you in your evening clothes."

"When you put it that way..." His warm lips brushed her neck, her jaw. "Maybe we could stay in Town for a bit. A few days alone together might do us some good."

She kissed his temple, but forced herself to draw back. Her body very much wanted to take the next logical step with her lawfully wedded husband, but their future together was still so uncertain.

Perhaps in London they could settle things between them.

"Yes," she agreed with a soft smile, "they might."

Chapter 8

JAMES AND CECILIA STAYED TWO more weeks with the Alstons, until His Grace could almost take a normal breath again. He was still weak and tired easily when they departed, but the rest of his symptoms seemed to have subsided. So, too, had Cecilia's apprehension—or, at least, that's the way it appeared to James.

They'd decided to share the large bed in their chamber and keep nighttime activities confined to sleeping only. Both of them had kept their promises faithfully, but James had been a little overwhelmed by the intimacy of lying in bed beside his wife. It wasn't just that they wore thin nightclothes and fewer layers than during the day, though that was part of it. For James, though, the simple act of being unconscious and the vulnerability that came with that was new. Who else could he be so completely unguarded with?

Who else could she trust with the same feeling?

Despite their firmness about falling asleep on opposite sides of the bed with plenty of empty space between them, James would often awaken with the sun to find Cecilia's back pressed against his. She never put her arms around him as she slept, but if he rolled over and cradled her in his, she would relax into his chest with a little sigh. He'd never felt such contentment wash through him as he had on those mornings.

And he couldn't wait to tell her she snored.

But he kept that bit of information to himself, trying valiantly to rein in his own apprehension. He hadn't been to a society event in seventeen years, and that had been a public assembly with other invitees from the untitled gentry like himself. The event they would be attending, Cecilia explained on the way to London, was the Marchioness of Whitby's Black and White Ball, the first major event of the Season each year. The ballroom would be decorated in black, white, and silver, as would the guests if they adhered to Lady Whitby's rule. And everyone important in society or government would be there, wondering who this upstart was and why he was bothering Lady Cecilia.

As luck would have it, though, Cecilia's niece and nephew-by-marriage were among the first people they found upon entering the Whitbys' ballroom on the appointed evening.

Honoria smiled when James bowed over her hand. "Uncle, how wonderful to see you here."

"We have one more item of business to attend to before I sweep your aunt away for an extended stay on the farm," he smiled back, slightly disappointed that there would be no hug from his new niece due to this public setting.

"How exciting!"

Cecilia laughed beside him, threading her arm through his. "Everything is an adventure to you, isn't it?"

Benedict took his wife's hand and grinned first at her, then at her aunt. "It is when you have the right company."

James glanced at his own wife and smiled. He'd originally planned to take her to the Fitzsimmons Farm after their betrothal when they were young, but that never happened. The circumstances were different now, but he discovered he was still looking forward to showing her his property, his livelihood.

And he very much wanted her to meet his family.

The couples parted after requesting dances from each of the ladies, and James escorted Cecilia around the perimeter of the ballroom.

"Lady Whitby outdid herself this year," Cecilia said, her eyes roaming around the room.

"Has she? I hadn't noticed." His voice was low and he waited until she met his gaze, then pointedly looked her up and down. She'd explained the details of her silver gown when they'd dressed earlier that evening, right down to the material making up what she'd called an overdress. But he saw none of it, only his lovely bride.

She swatted his arm, the tiniest hit of pink coloring her cheeks. "Am I so distracting?" she asked with half a laugh.

"You're beautiful," he answered without hesitation. She'd always been pretty, but tonight her eyes sparkled more brightly than ever despite her visible efforts to hold back a grin.

She leaned her head against his shoulder for an all-too-brief moment before murmuring, "Thank you." When she straightened again, she looked rather serious. "Will you kiss me for luck?"

"Here?" He'd kiss her anywhere she liked, but it was highly unfashionable to show affection to one's spouse in public. Kissing in the middle of a ballroom was unheard of.

"I don't want to lose my nerve."

Ah, she was worried about Grimsby. Cecilia had told James a bit of what she had planned for the blackmailing earl, and that she'd purposely left some of the encounter to chance. That, she'd confessed, made her slightly anxious.

"You'll be just fine," James said with a smile, laying his hand over hers as it rested on his arm. "No one wrongs Cecilia Maitland Fitzsimmons and escapes unscathed."

Her chin lifted and her grin returned. "You're absolutely right." Then she leaned in and brushed her soft lips across his cheek. "But a little luck never hurts."

She released his arm headed into the crowd —it was also highly unfashionable to be always together with one's spouse at a *ton* entertainment—leaving James on his own. He felt a wave of heat flood his body and suddenly didn't know what to do with his hands now that he had no wife to hold. But he took a deep breath and let it out slowly, nodding briefly at an older couple as they strolled past. If Cecilia could take on her blackmailer, James could get along in public without her for a while.

Cecilia couldn't remember the last time she was so tense at a ball—she was normally rather comfortable, even in the crush that was the Whitbys' Black and White Ball each year.

But she hadn't had a blackmailer to call out before.

Not that she was going to challenge him to a duel, of course. But she did plan to challenge his morality and honor before the entire assemblage. If she failed, if Grimsby was too clever to take the bait, then she could be the one humiliated.

And her husband and brother along with her.

But, oh, if she succeeded...

She smoothed her gloved hands down her cloth-of-silver skirt and set her shoulders, moving slowly but purposefully through the ballroom looking for Grimsby. She paused in her pursuit on occasion to talk to and be sociable with the other guests, trying to maintain a demeanor of gaiety as she would at any other entertainment. She circled the dancers and chaperones and gossiping dowagers, moved past the table laden with punch and lemonade, but the earl was nowhere to be found.

She tried the card room next, hiding a grin behind her fan when she spied James seated at a table with Lord Whitby. Her grin faded in the next instant, however. The Earl of Grimsby was slouching in a chair at the next table, his cards clutched in one hand against his black tailcoat.

"Ah, Grimsby!" Cecilia called, snapping her fan shut and waving it in his direction. "I've found you at last."

He started, straightening in his chair as his eyes widened for the briefest of moments. "Lady Cecilia, how nice to see you this evening. How might I be of service?"

She flitted across the room and halted at Grimsby's side, clasping her fan in both hands. "You've already done so much, finding that letter for me."

His brows rose a mere fraction of an inch. "Letter?"

"The letter I'd written to my dear husband so many years ago." She emphasized *husband* just a little, in case Grimsby hadn't heard about her recent marriage. Cecilia's man of business had forwarded a bank draft to the earl for the discharge of the loan against the Fitzsimmons

Farm. But she'd stood on principal and chosen not to give in to the blackmail and pay for the return of her letter.

Grimsby's brows rose to a loftier height, and Cecilia guessed that he hadn't known of her marriage to James. What fun that she be the one to inform him his scheme had no power over her any longer!

"Your husband?" Grimsby shook his head, then stood and gestured to the chair he had just vacated. "Why don't you sit, and we can discuss this matter without disturbing the other card players."

Cecilia ignored his suggestion and made sure her voice carried across the room. "I don't know how it could have gone missing—Mr. Fitzsimmons and I keep our private letters to each other in locked caskets—but I was enormously glad to receive your note detailing your possession of it."

Heads were turning throughout the card room, no doubt in response to her raised voice. But mouths opened and eyebrows were raised at her last statement. She could practically hear the other guests wondering how and why

Grimsby had obtained a personal letter belonging to a lady not his wife.

Grimsby shifted in his chair and started to speak but Cecilia cut him off, channeling her growing glee into her ruse. "I would also like to offer you a reward for your discretion, my lord. There are too many people in this world that would have used that letter to try to embarrass me or my family by threatening to make it public, but your only concern was making sure it was returned safely to me."

His expression froze in stony silence, and Cecilia couldn't tell if he was angry, or mortified, or some combination of emotions he'd rather not name. Whatever his feelings, she was absolutely delighted. She'd both exposed and negated his nefarious intentions without accusing him of anything at all.

"O-of course I cannot accept a reward," he managed, clenching his teeth with an audible *click*. "I am honor bound as a gentleman to return your property to you, and that I shall do."

Cecilia suppressed—with much difficulty— the urge to laugh. There went any money he'd hoped to extort from her, too. He could certainly try another private threat, but it would be a threat with no teeth. By appearing at the ball together, the whole of Polite Society now knew that Cecilia and James had wed, so there would be little if any scandal from a love letter between them. And by Grimsby's own admission to the entire card room, he had Cecilia's letter in his possession. If he refused to return it, she could simply ask him for it the next time she saw him...preferably in public.

"You are an honorable man, indeed, and I am grateful to you for keeping my letter safe."

His body seemed to deflate as he bowed to her. "I shall see to it first thing tomorrow."

She acknowledged his bow with a nod and turned, nodding to Lord Whitby and James. She'd intended to simply leave the room then, but James jumped to his feet and was at her side in three strides.

"We're both most appreciative, Lord Grimsby," James said with such sincerity Cecilia almost believed him.

Grimsby flashed a half-hearted smile, and when he declined to comment further, James offered Cecilia his arm. "Shall we, my dear? I believe the next dance belongs to me."

She slid her arm through his, drawing herself much closer to his side than was proper. "Yes, of course. My heart is so much lighter now with this business finally resolved."

She smiled broadly at her husband and allowed him to escort her out of the card room. When they'd cleared the door, James tugged her down the hall and into an open but empty room.

"Nicely played," he grinned, sliding his arms around her in a celebratory embrace.

She reciprocated, throwing her arms around his neck and pressing her cheek against his. "I wasn't sure it would work, but it did."

"You could talk anyone into anything, wife of mine," he murmured in her ear.

Cecilia closed her eyes, tightening her hold on him. "Flatterer," she whispered back with a smile. She held on for a moment longer, then loosened her grip on his shoulders. "Did you truly want to dance with me, or was that just an excuse to get away from Grimsby?"

"What I'd really like to do is return home and sit before a warm fire with you for a little while," he said, with a small smile. "We'll have to be up early tomorrow if we're going to make a good start toward the farm. I know you don't sleep well in a moving carriage."

"That sounds wonderful," she admitted. With her confrontation of her blackmailer concluded, she couldn't think of a reason to stay. "Though we can't leave until my letter arrives—Grimsby promised to send it first thing."

"Certainly not. We've gone to all this trouble to thwart the man, we may as well stay in Town long enough to see this matter concluded."

"My thoughts exactly."

He brushed his fingertips across her cheek and once again offered his arm. "To home, then, where we shall count down the minutes until your letter arrives."

Chapter 9

T O CECILIA'S SURPRISE, HER LETTER actually did arrive mid-morning the day after the ball, delivered by a footman in Grimsby livery. She unfolded the paper carefully and scanned the words to be sure it was *her* letter, then re-folded it and found it a place in her reticule where she could guard it closely.

By the time they reached the Fitzsimmons Farm, though, she'd forgotten all about her letter. There was so much to take in: the main house that was larger than her cousin Philip's home in the Cotswolds, the multitude of outbuildings, the adorable little lambs and foals, the friendliness of James's parents.

The biggest surprise, though, was a house tucked back in a corner of the property. Two stories high and built in red brick, it drew a grin from James that was so big Cecilia thought his face might split in two.

"This one is mine," he told her, throwing his arms wide. "The main house is where my parents lived when Father inherited this place, and where my sister and I spent our childhood. But when I came of age, I wanted something for my own."

"It's like a dower house," Cecilia replied with a wink, taking his offered hand as they circled the structure. "Except that the son of the family lives here rather than the dowager."

"Exactly. The property still officially belongs to my father, and this was a way for me to have some privacy and autonomy until the day comes when I inherit."

He escorted her through the interior, pointing out structural features he'd requested and the decorating he'd done himself, all with that wide grin.

"It's very cozy, James. And I don't mean that as a euphemism for 'small' either—this house looks to be the same size as my home in Hanover Square. And every room feels like a place I'd enjoy spending time." She squeezed his hand gently. "You clearly do."

"I do," he echoed. "My parents keep talking about moving out of the main house and giving it over to me, but I keep telling them not to. I'm more than happy here."

They stopped before the entrance to an empty room on the ground floor, and Cecilia peered inside. "Why haven't you furnished this room?"

"I was saving it as a sitting room for my eventual wife."

His words were even in tone and volume, but his eyes locked onto hers as he spoke. All she could manage in response was, "Oh." She released his hand and clasped hers together. "We probably ought to—"

"James? Are you in here?" a female voice called from the front door.

"Mother?"

Cecilia followed her husband back through the house toward the door and discovered Mrs. Fitzsimmons standing in the entry.

"There you are," she smiled at her son. "Your steward is looking for you, and I was hoping to show Lady Cecilia some of the duties belonging to the lady of the manor."

Cecilia shared a look with James and gave him a small nod. Finding out how the farm worked was one of the reasons she'd wanted to make this trip. "That would be lovely, Mrs. Fitzsimmons. And you must call me Cecilia. I am family now, no matter how that came to be."

She felt warm pressure on her hand and James flashed her a smile. "I'll leave you two, then."

Cecilia spent the rest of the afternoon shadowing her mother-in-law as she went about her daily routine. As James had told her at Orchard Lake, there was little difference between running a large farm and a small estate. The Fitzsimmons Farm employed fewer servants inside the house than Alston did at any one of his country estates, but they're number included the usual housekeeper and butler, along with a variety of maids and a few footmen. The kitchen garden was larger than Cecilia's in Town and Mrs. Fitzsimmons was more involved with the care of hers than Cecilia, but that, too, was familiar.

"All these years I thought being a farmer's wife would be completely foreign to me," Cecilia smiled after they'd gone over the dinner menu with the cook. "Yet, the things you've shown me here today are the things I do in my own home."

"It was different for James's great-grandparents," Mrs. Fitzsimmons responded. "The farm was smaller then, and so was the income it produced. They employed one maid-of-all-work and a few field hands, but that was all. When I married Mr. Fitzsimmons, I thought that's what I was walking into, myself."

"Were you terrified?"

Mrs. Fitzsimmons giggled. "I was. My mother-in-law had gone on to her reward before I came here, and Mr. Fitzsimmons's grandmother was in ill health, so I had no one to show me what to do."

"I would have been overwhelmed," Cecilia said softly.

"Oh no," Mrs. Fitzsimmons replied quickly. "I am a gentleman's daughter and managed without too much trouble. You, having been raised in grander circumstances than I, would have made this house your own in short order."

"I suppose I would have." She glanced around Mrs. Fitzsimmons's sitting room with its oak escritoire and chairs upholstered in powder blue, thinking of that empty room in James's house. Would she choose different fabric for her chairs? A different wood for her writing desk? Would James sit with her in the evenings and discuss the day's business while she embroidered?

"Thank you for taking me under your wing," Cecilia smiled. "If there is nothing else for today, I believe I'll lie down for a while before dinner. For all the traveling I do, I still haven't managed to learn how to sleep well in the carriage."

"Of course. Do you remember the way?"

"I can just follow the path, can't I?"

Mrs. Fitzsimmons's eyes widened. "Yes, if you were going to James's house. Your chamber is upstairs. We assumed that since yours was a marriage of convenience..."

"I see. Well, then, upstairs I shall go."

There was an unexpected twist. After spending weeks upon weeks with James—including a few coaching inns with only one room available—she was to finally have her privacy back.

But did she want it?

James lay in bed that night and tried to sleep, but his eyes remained open and his mind alert. He thought that, between the fitful sleep he managed traveling from London and tramping all around the farm this afternoon, he'd be falling asleep in his supper. But here he was in his own bed at last, with the familiar sounds of his home around him, and he remained wide awake.

"Well, if I'm not going to sleep, then I should do something useful," he said aloud, swinging his legs over the side of the bed. He found a pair of trousers to put on and grabbed a clean shirt from his clothespress, pulling it on as he moved through the moonlit house. A pair of thick stockings his mother had knitted for him completed his ensemble and warmed his icy feet.

He decided to tackle the stack of correspondence that had piled up in his absence, taking out a fresh sheet of paper as he opened the topmost letter. Before he could read a word, he was startled by a noise at the front of the house.

Was someone knocking?

When he opened the door, he was greeted by the sight of his wife bundled in what his mother liked to call a wrapper, her bright hair hanging in a thick braid over her shoulder.

"Cecilia? What are you doing here at this time of night?"

"Perhaps we could discuss it inside? Spring may have come to England, but you'd never know it this night."

He shook himself and held the door wider for her. "Of course. I'm afraid the only fire laid is in my bedchamber, though. Do you mind talking there?"

She smirked at him as she entered the house, twining her arm around his. "How scandalous, Mr. Fitzsimmons! Whatever will the neighbors think if they find out?"

"Let us hope we never have to find out," he replied with mock seriousness. "This way, my lady."

When she was seated before the fire and suitably comfortable, James tried again. "To what do I owe this pleasure, Wife?"

"Is it a pleasure, Husband?" she asked softly.

How was he supposed to answer that? "I have only spent two days with you that were not somehow pleasurable: the day you refused my proposal, and the day you proposed to me."

"Do you mean that?"

The firelight was flickering over her face, illuminating it one moment and plunging it into shadow the next, making it difficult to read her expression. There was no other chair in the room for him to sit in, so he knelt before her and took her hands in his.

"Yes."

She let out a breath as if she'd been holding it, awaiting his answer. "Do you think... Do you think we might have more pleasurable days together?"

His mouth pulled into a wide grin. "I certainly hope so." Her answering grin made his heart flutter in his chest.

"Good. Because I believe we've been given a second chance, my love, and I am loath to squander it. Lying in bed tonight, it was all I could think about. Now that you're back in your own home and the farm is safe, you don't need me any longer. My letter is returned and my brother spared the stress of a scandal, so I don't need you any longer, either."

James felt his face fall. Could she see his disappointment in the dark room? "I suppose not," he replied, keeping his voice as neutral as he was able.

She squeezed his hands and drew them into her lap. "But just because we are no longer dependent upon each other doesn't mean this is the end of our relationship."

"Do you want this to be the end?" He couldn't keep the emotion out of his voice now. Not when his future was being decided, when her chilly hands were warming his very heart.

"No," she said resolutely, releasing his hands and fished around in the pocket of her wrapper. When her hand emerged, it was holding a folded letter with her own faded handwriting. "But I don't think we can have this again, either."

He took the letter when she offered it, sitting back on his heels as his eyes roaming over the old paper. It was a letter she'd written to him during their courtship, not long before he'd asked for her hand, filled with florid descriptions of her love and longing for him. He remembered penning similar letters to her, and how he ached for her when they were apart for more than a few moments.

"I believe you're right about this," he said, gesturing with the letter. "This is not who we are anymore."

"Precisely. But my dearest James, we've already begun forging a new path—together—and I want very much to continue along it with you. Will you stay with me, and remain my husband?"

"On one condition."

He heard her suck in a breath. "What?"

"That you move into this house with me for the remainder of our stay here. We may no longer be young, but I still miss you when we're apart."

She slid from her seat and caught him in a warm embrace. "I believe I can meet that condition."

She kissed him then, with such enthusiasm that the pair of them toppled over. James couldn't stop the laughter, but wrapped his arms around his wife sprawled atop him and managed a few more kisses.

"I love you, Cecilia Fitzsimmons. I have since the day I first laid eyes on you, and I always will."

She rubbed her nose against his, then claimed his lips once more. "And I love you, James Fitzsimmons. I have made some mistakes along the way, and we have had more than our share of heartbreak because of it. But I promise to keep loving you as best I can for as long as I live."

She bent to kiss him again and he rolled them over, propping himself up on one elbow as he looked down into her eyes. "I will hold you to that promise, wife of mine."

Cecilia's answering smile shone almost brighter than the fire. She ran her fingers through his hair and massaged his neck. "You'd better."

Later, when they were cuddled up together in James's bed, Cecilia planted a kiss on his shoulder. "How are we going to manage this?"

"I thought we managed rather well," he grinned back.

To his delight, she laughed. "Yes, I think we did. But that's not what I meant. We have two different lives; yours is here, while mine is mostly in London. I'm happy to spend time here, of course, but you've been so anxious leaving the farm in someone else's hands."

He took a deep breath, studying his wife as she braced her arms on his chest and pushed herself up. She'd spent her share of time in the country, and he had no doubt she'd be happy here. But she'd been so at home in London, and he knew how much she enjoyed the whirl of the social season.

"The steward acquitted himself decently," James allowed, brushing her long hair behind her shoulder. "With Father here to keep an eye on him, I could steel my nerves enough to leave the farm."

"Truly?"

The hope in her eyes helped him warm to the idea. "Certainly. We can make our home here most of the year and spend the summer in Town for the Season. It's a bit far from your brother, but not prohibitively so."

What he didn't say was that, if Cecilia were summoned to Alston's death bed, she might not make it in time from the Fitzsimmons Farm. But he suspected she already realized that. And she might be too far away no matter where—or with whom—she was.

"Sounds like you've put some thought into this plan of yours." She caressed his cheek with her fingertips. "Thank you for that."

"What will it be, then, my lady? Can you see your way to a rural life?"

He held his breath, not even caring how obvious it was with her lying on his chest.

"How could I not?" she said, smiling softly in the firelight. I've waited all these years for a second chance with you, my love. I'm not about to let you go now."

James wrapped Cecilia in his arms and kissed her hair. "That, my dear, is music to my ears.

Ready for more Maitland Maidens? Read on for a sneak peek...

Kissing by the Mistletoe

Maitland Maidens Book 3

Chapter 1

Kent, England
December 1813

MADDIE HAYWARD PERCHED ON THE edge of her chair in Mrs. Spencer's drawing room, back straight, dark hair neatly pinned up, politely smiling as she sipped from a tea cup painted with delicate pink and yellow flowers.

"I understand the Mathisons will be visiting your family for a few weeks," Mrs. Spencer announced.

The other ladies in the room tittered and Maddie fought to keep her smile from slipping. "That's right."

"Mrs. Mathison and…both her sons?" someone else asked, not quite able to sound nonchalant.

Maddie suppressed the urge to roll her eyes. Kit Mathison, the oldest son, had been Maddie's best friend for years—since before his father died and his mother had taken her children to Edinburgh, where her brother lived. Because Kit was handsome, unattached, and possessed a comfortable income, Maddie was supposed to be in love with him.

She did love him, but as the brother she never had, not as a potential husband. Yet whenever she corrected people's assumptions, her words were dismissed. Apparently no one could conceive of a gentleman and a lady maintaining a close friendship without designs on each other.

"Yes," Maddie responded, hoping no one else heard the slight edge in her voice. "Kit and Thomas will both be accompanying their mother."

"You're so lucky," a younger woman sighed. "How wonderful would it be to dance with Kit Mathison?"

Maddie smiled at that with genuine goodwill. Dancing with the local women was something Kit had mentioned in his last letter. It was one of the things he was most looking forward to. "Perhaps you'll have the chance at the assembly this week. I know for a fact that he's eager to see everyone."

Mrs. Spencer waved her hand reprovingly, but let out a little chuckle. "Miss Hayward, you shouldn't tease. We are all aware to whom Mr. Mathison will be directing his attention."

And there was the other side of the coin—Kit was also reputed to be in love with Maddie.

For his part, Kit was highly amused by the whole situation. The consequences were less severe for him, though. Ladies still swooned over him, and not one would decline his addresses. Maddie, being female, was at a disadvantage: she was supposed to try to attract a gentleman and wait for him to initiate a courtship. But no true gentleman would encroach on what he saw as another man's dominion.

Which left Maddie in a precarious position. She had few practical skills, no wealthy family, and little money of her own. If she failed to marry, her only option was to remain in her parents' home and find some way to contribute to the household, lest she become a burden to them.

She smiled as best she could at Mrs. Spencer, feeling her resistance fade away. There wasn't any use in arguing when no one listened to the argument. "But he can't be by my side all the time."

With Maddie's seeming acceptance of the situation, the ladies of the drawing room beamed at her. Then they changed the subject, and no one spoke to Maddie directly for the rest of the visit.

"How does Mrs. Spencer?" Maddie's mother asked when she returned home. "Did she carry on about her new teacups the way I thought she would?"

"She looked well," Maddie answered, removing her bonnet and smoothing down her hair. "She was very keen on the new teacups, yes, but they weren't the focus of our conversation."

Her mother grinned. "I'm sure I know what was, though. How many ladies asked after Kit?"

This time Maddie let her eyes roll. Not that she didn't expect it from her mother, but she'd been hoping they might get through one day without an allusion to her supposed relationship with Kit.

Apparently it wasn't this day. "They all did, at one point or another."

"You are a lucky girl," her mother said, echoing the sentiments of the drawing room ladies. "To think, in just a few weeks' time you could be Mrs. Christopher Mathison."

"What?"

"Surly he'll make you a pretty proposal at Christmas, with both families here to celebrate."

Maddie's mother was practically glowing at the thought of her daughter marrying the head of the Mathison family. Misplaced though it was, Maddie didn't have the heart to shatter the illusion. Everyone would settle down again when Christmas came and went with no proposal of marriage from Kit. And if she truly was lucky, he would find the right woman and marry her. Quickly.

She kissed her mother's cheek and headed to her bedchamber, putting her bonnet in its usual place in her battered wardrobe. What if Kit didn't marry quickly? How long could she linger with the wallflowers and chaperones at every event, unseen by gentlemen who might otherwise have taken an interest in her?

What if he didn't marry at all?

The thought nearly knocked the breath out of her. All Maddie had ever wanted was to have a home and children of her own, to share her life with a man she adored. If Kit remained unattached, would everyone continue to think of her as his? Would she slip into spinsterhood while the eligible bachelors of Kent looked elsewhere?

Maddie dropped onto her bed, bracing her hands against the pomegranate red counterpane her grandmother had brought with her from Spain when she'd married Maddie's grandfather. What would she have done in this situation?

Maddie laid back and grinned. Gran would have flouted convention and begun asking gentlemen to dance and drive and walk out with her. Maddie wasn't quite so bold, but perhaps there was something she could do to take control of her life—this aspect of it, at least. Perhaps Kit would have some ideas, or maybe his brother, Thomas, could help.

She pictured Thomas as she'd last seen him, tall and lanky, his reddish hair curling every which way when he didn't try to tame it with pomade. That had been the last time he'd visited the Haywards, right before he went off to university three years ago. He'd always been kind to her, quick to offer a helping hand when she'd needed one.

Of course, she'd only ever needed his assistance exiting a carriage or his company walking into the village. But Thomas was clever. If he and Kit and Maddie put their heads together, she was certain they'd come up with some way to uncouple her from Kit's non-existent romantic attachment.

Thomas Mathison sat on the rear-facing seat in his brother's traveling coach, his eyes drifting out the window to watch the scenery roll past as he wiped his palms on his trousers. He'd been looking forward to this visit since Mrs. Hayward proposed the idea two months ago, but the closer they drew to the Haywards' home, the more frenzied the butterflies in his stomach became. He had corresponded some with Maddie in the years since they'd last seen each other, so it wasn't as if they'd be strangers after so much time apart. But what if things had changed for her that she hadn't mentioned in her letters? Was she still interested in gardening? Still fleet of foot when skating on the little pond near the village?

An image of ice skating with Maddie formed in his mind, as clear as if it had happened only moments ago: Maddie skating backward, bundled up against the cold, holding Thomas's hands as he drew her closer with promises to keep her warm. She wrapped her arms around his neck and lifted her face for his kiss, and he obliged with a grin.

One of the carriage wheels rolled over a rock and Thomas's head bumped against the window, dissolving the image. Maddie undoubtedly thought of him as Kit's little brother and nothing else. Perhaps she was even skating with—and being warmed by—someone else, even as the geographical gap between them was closing. The thought pierced his heart and he had to stifle a grunt of pain.

Not that he had any claim on her. He had thought it prudent to wait until he'd found work and saved up enough money to support a wife before he spoke to Maddie of love and marriage. He smoothed his hands over his thighs, attempting to wipe away the sweat that was forming again on his palms. Maybe it would be better if Maddie found someone else, someone who wouldn't have to worry about whether or not he could afford a home and clothing and food for more than just himself. She deserved to be with a man who could take care of her, who could give her not only the things she needed but everything she wanted.

"Thomas, dear, are you all right?"

He turned to his mother, sitting opposite him, and blinked. "Yes, I'm quite well."

"Are you certain? It sounded as though you'd hit your head rather hard."

He heard a quiet chuckle from Kit's side of the carriage. "Don't worry mother. Thomas's head is hard enough to withstand a little bump."

Thomas smirked at his brother. "Not as hard as yours, of course. Didn't you once get hit by a mallet and keep right on walking?" Thomas knew very well about the mallet—he'd been holding it when it had bashed Kit in the temple. Accidentally, of course.

Kit grinned and rapped his knuckles against his skull. "Sturdy as a block of marble."

"I do hope the two of you won't be acting like adolescents in the presence of the Haywards," their mother sighed. "Maddie Hayward will not look fondly on a man who cannot put his boyhood behind him."

Kit laughed. "Maddie is the one who gave Thomas the mallet, mother."

Their mother pressed her lips together for a moment before saying, "Yes, but that was years ago. I'm sure she's become a well-behaved young lady now, and if you want to pay your addresses to her, you ought to consider your own behavior."

It was a common refrain among the Mathisons, that Kit and Maddie would settle down together someday. No one but Kit knew of the hope Thomas harbored regarding Maddie, and that was the way he preferred it. But it still stung to have that hope so easily dashed by his own mother.

"I will promise to behave myself," Kit said, patting his mother's hand as it lay on the seat between them. "But I will not promise to court Maddie, no matter how many times you imply that I want to."

"There's no harm in wanting to spend time with her again before you ask for her hand," their mother smiled. "But you can't have been so close to her all these years without meaning to marry her."

"I can, Mother. And I have."

"What about me?" Thomas blurted out. "I've been close to her, too. Might it be possible that I want to marry her?"

He could feel his cheeks warming, and hoped he wasn't actually blushing. His mother was studying his face as if he might be, but then she shook her head.

"Your relationship with her isn't like Kit's. I know that you're fond of her, but she has always spent more time with your brother. She confides in him."

Thomas knew that was true, but felt himself frowning nonetheless. "You don't think Maddie could ever be interested in me?"

His mother reached across the carriage and took his hand for a moment. "I know that there are several ladies in Edinburgh who have already set their caps for you, my sweet boy— your uncle has told me as much. You've been the toast of his social circle since you arrived, he said, and you'll have scores of women to choose from when you're ready to take a wife."

Thomas could see the pride in her eyes, in the set of her mouth, and it warmed him.

"But," she went on, "Maddie was meant for Kit."

Kit crossed his arms over his chest with a frown, but didn't protest. Thomas wasn't surprised—the family joke about hard-headedness didn't just apply to the two brothers. Their mother could be absolutely single-minded when it came to certain subjects, and arguing with her was often a fruitless occupation.

He went back to his window, noting the addition of a few darker clouds among the puffy white ones. He came back to the idea that it might be better if Maddie did have a beau. That would leave Kit free of their mother's expectations and allow Thomas to put aside a dream that would likely never come true. He'd only have to deal with the pain of seeing her with someone else for a few weeks, then he could get on with the business of living without her. One day, he might even find contentment with one of the ladies his mother had mentioned.

Yes, that would be the easiest way out of this dilemma. He would simply ignore the possibility of impending heartbreak.

Other Books by Cora Lee

<u>Sweet & Traditional:</u>
Save the Last Dance for Me (Maitland Maidens #1)
Back In My Arms Again (Maitland Maidens #2)
Kissing by the Mistletoe (Maitland Maidens #3)
A Kiss to Build a Dream On (Maitland Maidens #4)
When I Fall In Love (Maitland Maidens #5)

<u>Spicy Novellas:</u>
What If I Loved You

<u>Spicy and Suspenseful:</u>
No Rest for the Wicked
The Good, The Bad, And The Scandalous
The Duke of Darkness

About the Author

Cora Lee is a National Bestselling author of Regency romance. She went on a twelve year expedition through the blackboard jungle as a high school math teacher before publishing *Save the Last Dance for Me*, the first book in the Maitland Maidens series. She then followed it up with eight other novels and novellas ranging from sweet and traditional to spicy and suspenseful.

When she's not walking Rotten Row at the fashionable hour or attending the entertainments of the Season, you might find her participating in Regency Fiction Writers events, wading through her towering TBR pile, or eagerly awaiting the next Marvel movie release. If you'd like to find out more about Cora or her books you can visit her website, sign up for her newsletter, or connect with her on Facebook, Bookbub, or Goodreads.